Chairman of Fools

Chairman of Fools

Shimmer Chinodya

WEAVER
—PRESS—

Published by Weaver Press, Box A1922, Avondale, Harare, 2005.

© Shimmer Chinodya
Typeset by Weaver Press
Cover Design: Xealos
Printed by Bardwell Printers, Harare

The publishers would like to express their gratitude to Hivos for
the support they have given to Weaver Press in the development of
their fiction programme.

The author would like to express his gratitude to the Civitella
Rainieri Centre, Umbertide, Italy for awarding him a fellowship in
August 2004 which enabled him to write this book.

ISBN: 1 77922 041 3
ISBN-13: 978 1 77922 041 0

The author acknowledges the following musicians and songs
quoted in the novel:

Brenda Fassie – Weekend Special

Harare Mambos – Kudendere

Tina Turner – I don't want to fight no more

Thomas Mapfumo – Joyce

Stevie Wonder – (Unnamed)

Peter Gabriel – Don't give up

Bruce Springsteen – Born in the USA

Simply Red – Fair-ground

Sankomota – Stop the war

B.B.King – Hold On

Ray Phiri – Can't spend your life just taking

Shimmer Chinodya was born in Gweru in 1957 and educated in Zimbabwe. On completion of his first degree he went to the Iowa Writers Workshop where he did an MA in Creative Writing. His publications include the novels *Dew in the Morning* (1982), *Farai's Girls* (1984), *Child of War* (1985), under his pen-name, Ben Chirasha, *Harvest of Thorns* (1989), an anthology, *Can We Talk and other stories* (1998) and a teenage novella, *Tale of Tamari* (2004). *Harvest of Thorns* won the Commonwealth Writers Prize (Africa region) in 1990; *Can We Talk* was shortlisted for the Caine Prize in 2000. Chinodya has also written children's books under his pen-name, as well as the script for the award-winning feature film, *Everyone's Child*. In addition, he has developed a highly acclaimed language textbook series: *Step Ahead: New Secondary English Course*. Chinodya has won many fellowships abroad and from 1995-97 was visiting professor in Creative Writing and African Literature at the University of St Lawrence in the USA. Chinodya works as a free-lance writer and consultant.

Glossary

baba – father

babamukuru – father's brother/husband's brother

bhudhi – brother

blaz – slang for brother

buda ndibudewo – literally 'come out (of mother's womb) sibling, so that I can come out too'

chikafu – food

chinamwari – a ritual practised in south and central Africa to prepare young women for better sex, wifely duties and motherhood

chiramu – playful but innocent way in which young in laws from the related families act as 'wives 'and 'husbands' to each other

combi – a mini-bus used as a public taxi

futi futi – and, and

gogo – grandmother

guru – offal, tripe

hakata – the diviner's bones

hes mhani – hie there!

Hesi mhani – oh, yeah!

hwindi – conductor in a combi taxi

iwe – you

kanga – roasted maize grains

kanjani – how is it?

kaya – servants' quarters in suburban yards

kuchirungu – the city; in this particular context, the USA

kumusha – rural areas

kutyei – why not?

kwakanaka here – is everything all right?

maakunzwa sei – how are you feeling now?

mabva nekupi – where are you coming from?

mabhoyi – half-derogatory name for black people

madora – a type of edible caterpillar

mai – mother of

maiguru – mother's older sister/brother's wife/wife's older sister

mainini – mother's younger sister, or wife's younger sister

majuru – a type of ant, edible when fried

makadii – how are you?

makadii mhamha – how are you mother,/mother–in–law?

mamuka sei – how are you this morning?

manheru – good evening
matumbu – offal, intestines
mazhanje – a sweet wild fruit, a wild loquat
mazondo – boiled cow hooves
mbuya – grandmother, aunt
mhaiwe – oh, Mother! Exclamation of surprise, pain, etc.
mhamha – mother/mum/mother-in-law
mkoma – brother, usually older brother
mkwasha – brother-in-law/son-in-law
mombes – cattle
munin'ina – young brother or sister
mupfuwira – love potion to bait loved man/woman
muramu – wife's younger sister or husband's younger brother
muri bho? – are you OK?
muzukuru – grandchild/ nephew/niece
mwana vamaivangu – my mother's child/sibling
mwanangu – my son
namatambudziko – condolences
nhaika – OK?
palazzo – knee length shorts
sascams – Zimbabwean slang for mentally disturbed people
sekuru – grandfather, uncle, older man worthy of respect
sisi – sister
shebeen – private 'bar', usually in a private house
tsano – brother-in-law
vabereki – parents
vatezvara – father-in-law
waswera – How was your day?
wena uzaba u – Ndebele for 'You will be...'
zambias – light, cotton wrappers worn by African women, so called
because they are popular in Zambia
zvako – lucky you
zvauriwe – watch yourself
zvekuti – very much
zvigure – traditional masked dancers belonging to certain cults

1

And what is it, my dear husband, that's eating you up? What is it that's making you hate yourself, hate me? Can't you see that this phoney, artsy life of yours is hurting you, harming me and dragging your children and everybody around you into the steep-sided pits of your despair? You are keeping bad company; your image badly needs sprucing up, you have to be schooled again in the simple ways of trust. The word SELFISH is branded on your forehead, like numbers scorched onto the flanks of mindless cattle. You brook no advice; you have mangled your sense of time and scratched the word 'purpose' out of the grammar of your habits. A year out there, after a decade of blame and abuse and you think I'll take it forever. You think I'll stay the same, that I won't change to become ME, MYSELF, I, ME. Be warned, my dear man, that I'm definitely changing; that there are things in store for you...

When Farai arrives home he finds Veronica asleep. Her left arm hangs limply out of the sheets, her wedding ring gleaming faintly in the moonlight that is filtering into the bedroom through the high, curtainless windows. He wanders into the study to look for mail and messages, and then into the kitchen for a bite, but finding nothing prepared, brushes his teeth and climbs carefully into bed beside her. Something, perhaps a large rat, makes a strange, thumping movement in the ceiling but he is too tipsy to worry about it. For hours he cannot rest. Lately, alcohol has not brought him the deep sleep he so badly needs. He shudders at the thought of the binges that characterised the last few weeks before his return home.

In the morning she startles him awake with her hair drier.

'Why don't you try natural locks?' he says, sleepily, longingly. She is wearing a new white cheese-cloth dress with buttons all the way up the front and black high heels. She sprays a subtle perfume under her arms and between her thighs. He feels envious of her and yet angry with her. A woman can change a lot in twenty short months.

He sits up and reaches for her.

'No,' she pushes his arms away. 'If you had wanted that you would have come home earlier.'

'You left me no supper.'

'If you'd wanted food as well, you'd have been here earlier still.'

'Some men come home to find supper waiting for them.'

'Men who respect their wives and families.'

'But I've only been back three days.'

'So you're already trying to catch up on what you missed. Back to your old ways. What about me, alone here, with the children?'

'You make it sound as if I was over there having a picnic.'

'Why didn't you take us with you?'

'We've been over this a hundred times. Why should I drag my family into all that snow and snobbery when I've built a nest for them here? Squandering a fortune? To prove what?'

'It would've been a good experience for the children.'

'Would you have left your job for two years of nonsense, and then come back to find new school places for the children and work for yourself? You're too ambitious for that.'

'One can always begin a new career. We're not working to buy an aeroplane, you know. One day you'll die and leave your estate to be devoured by wolves. We won't see a cent of it. You should learn to spend your money while you are still alive.'

'You take for granted all the little comforts I starve myself to create for you.'

'Don't exaggerate. You're full of self-pity and you just worship money.'

'No, you do. Secretly. You contradict yourself. On the one hand you preach thrift but on the other you are obsessed with the image of wealth and prosperity held up by your church. You're envious of me. The real trouble is you think I was over there having fun.'

'How can I think otherwise when you start your disappearing act as soon as you set foot at home?'

'What d'you expect me to do when go to that church of yours three times a day?'

'Maybe I've found comfort in it. Maybe it's time I became my real self, and stopped you trying to change me into whoever you want me to be.'

'We've gone through this a thousand times. I wish ...'

'There you go again. Talking, talking and listening to yourself and blaming me for everything. That's what you have done all your life. I can't stand it any more. Now take your hands off my dress. I'm late already.'

'What about breakfast?'

'You've been making that for yourself for ten months, or so you say. Remember, when you phoned home you promised us a surprise breakfast one day. Why don't you try that today?'

Veronica picks up her bag, her bible and the car keys and swishes out of the bedroom. The children, Sharai, eight, and Ticha, six, are waiting for her in the passage, decked out in their new clothes. Their first daughter, Rumbi, is a high school boarder in the mountains four hours away.

He slips on his gown and follows them to the door. There is no time for good mornings, just the clinking of keys as at a jail-room door. He watches from the window as Veronica drives out through the electric gate in her blue Corolla, the exhaust of the car rattling. Switching off the DSTV left on by the children, he enters the kitchen to find out if there is anything to eat. The fridge is full of meat, bread, vegetables, milk and the pantry shelves are well stocked with eggs, rice, spaghetti, sugar, maize meal, cooking oil and fruit juice, but he has no appetite, nor the strength or desire to cook. A hangover throbs at his temples. Maybe he should just have an ice cold beer but god no, this is a Christian house and drinking is taboo. Veronica would never allow it, let alone buy him a beer. When they first married there was always a beer or two in the fridge but nowadays, especially since she joined the new church, he is uncomfortable drinking at home. When he has visitors, and these are rare, he has to rush to the shops to buy drinks.

In the lounge he picks up the framed photograph of his late mother. She stares out at him. He is surprised to remember how young she was when she died – only fifty-three – ravaged by cancer and bedridden in this very house under his youthful, unknowing care. His photogenic father, struck dead by a sudden stroke at seventy, had left no photographs worth framing. Nor had Dzimai, his taciturn brother whose fate he hated to recall and for whom he hadn't shed a tear.

Mooching into the study, Farai stares at the telephone. Damn it, Piri the dancer had said she had no phone, and he had not been sober or focussed for long enough to get a specific address, or to find out what she would be doing today. 'It's funny,' he thinks, 'how those precious names and numbers salted away in bulging purses or glove lockers have the knack of disappearing, just when they are most needed.'

***

He bathes, puts on a clean change of clothes, locks up the house, and like a dazed, deodorised assailant, drives out to assault the city. His old Mazda 323 is still a good runner – he plans to buy a new model once his overseas stint is finally over. One more year out there, alone, is a long time. Again he wonders why he accepted the job.

While he is filling up at the local garage who should pull up but Wilbert, the only man he can perhaps claim as a real friend, as their friendship goes back to their schooldays nearly three decades ago. They studied together in the hockey fields, picked *mazhanje* in the forest and raided neighbouring farmers' maize fields for *kanga* on full moonlit nights. Wilbert is now the quintessential family man, marrying off brothers, chastising errant sisters' husbands, burying clansmen and overseeing enormous weddings. Modest Wilbert, now a financial director, but still trundling up in his old pick-up truck with a little boy on the front seat. Within seconds Farai, laughing, bursts out of his car to give Wilbert a hug.

'Man! Hey! When did you get back?' The months slip away in a few jokes and Wilbert invites him to have 'one one' at a nearby bottle store. His friend volunteers little about his life besides bemoaning the rigours of work and domestication and the approaching mid-forties. Farai knows Wilbert envies him his freer career and ability to travel. He talks expansively about his experiences in America, his problems with Veronica, and with drink, but he says little about the women cluttering his life.

'You ought to eat before you go drinking, Farai. And try going to church with the missus and the babies once in a while.'

Wilbert's advice sounds mundane; the kind gleaned at smoky barbeques and crowded bottle stores. Most men don't take advice easily, even from friends. But they like to drink together all the same. 'One one' becomes 'two two' and 'two two' becomes 'three three' and 'three three' often becomes 'four four'. Wilbert typically refuses to allow Farai to pay. The baby is fidgeting on the seat and has had enough chips and Fantas and his wife Clara must be wondering where he is with the milk, tomatoes and potatoes. He has to go. He leaves with promises of a further meeting tomorrow afternoon, when he is free.

Left alone, Farai ponders his fate. He has money, and time to kill, but no one to spend it with. The beer so early in the day is exhilarating him but intensifies his loneliness. He thinks perhaps he should have a small house, but he has never had the patience to run one nor a woman to try it out with. Besides, he has never been a small house man. He fears attachment. He is a man waiting to be found; a confused being waiting to be rediscovered and restored to himself. He hops from pub to pub, jesting with women, arguing with old acquaintances and is somewhat amazed at how adept he is becoming at it. He frequents the pubs in search of familiarity and security but after five pints he feels no better.

At one of his roadside haunts a leggy woman in her mid-twenties, wearing a black dress and purple doek, plants herself on a free chair, opposite him across a cement table.

'Fatima!'

'I thought you'd forgotten me. When did you come back?'

'Three days ago. How did you know I was away?'

'It was in the papers. And you told me before you left. How was it?'

'So-so.'

'You said you would write to me. You probably tore up my address even before you boarded the plane. You have too many of us all over the place. When are you ever going to grow up and settle down?'

'Cheers! To my ancestors! What are you doing here?'

'Just having fun.'

'Are you looking for men?'

'Of course not.'

'Are you married now?'

'Heavens, no.'

'How is your little boy?'

'He's going to school now, in Grade 1. And how's your wife?'

'She's OK.'

'She must be happy you're back. You should spend more time with her and your children. Is she still going to that new church of hers?'

'Zvekuti!'

'Perhaps it's good for you to have such a wife. You don't realise it, but you need her. Make sure you don't lose her.'

'You're gaining weight. Are you sure you aren't pregnant?'

'Who gets pregnant these days with funny diseases around and tonnes of condoms at every street corner?'

'Or perhaps you're eating lots of fish?'

'Oh, fish. You love fish. Fish is good for you. Fish is innocent. Pork is bad. Never, ever, eat pork in people's houses, especially at night. Remember that weird day soon after you buried your father and came crawling to my compound when all the bars closed, caked with dirt and shaking with hunger and I cooked you a big fresh bream from the dam and you put up in my room, and in the morning I soaped and scrubbed you up in my little grass bathroom and you wore my *palazzo* while I washed and ironed your clothes?'

'Yeah.'

'I wonder why your wife let you go out like that.'

'She's too educated.'

'Who says educated women should treat their husbands that way?'

'She never went to *chinamwari* like you did.'

'In my country even women with university degrees take traditional courses in looking after their husbands.'

'One day I'll thank you for looking after me then.'

'And yet you brought me nothing. Are you back for good?'

'I'm going back for another year.'

'Don't bring us back a skinny little white woman who is too scared to kill a fowl.'

'No, I won't. I love black women. Hey, that big bream – was that the day we woke up and went to see *zvigure*, the masked dancers from Malawi?'

'No, that was another day. New year, two years ago. You drank non-stop without sleeping for two days, and talked all night. A woman next door heard you and she said she knew a man who might be able to help you. A traditional healer.'

'What makes you think I need help?'

'I can tell. When did you last eat?'

'Yesterday morning.'

'Are you hungry?'

'Not really.'

'How many crates of beer have you taken?'

'Maybe a half.'

'Do you want to go and see *zvigure* now?'

'Yeah, why not? Where?'

'At a farm not far from here.'

'OK.'

'Can we pick up my friend Enesi on the way? She's my home girl. I know you love going out with two women.'

'Do I?'

'Just don't get too carried away like you did last time we went with Rakeri.'

***

At sunset Farai sits ensconced between Fatima and Enesi drinking and watching *zvigure*. Enesi is a lean dark girl with a good laugh. The place, an old tobacco barn, is full of cheering men, women and children. A dozen or so smart cars are parked outside and Farai waves at a well-dressed woman he thinks he was at university with, one who was in Veronica's class. He is surprised to see her here. The dancers are all male with grass skirts, brightly coloured blouses, hideously painted masks and wild wigs of imitation Caucasian hair. They are mounted on incredibly tall stilts and take turns to twist, gyrate and incite the crowd with a blur of suggestive motions. The drums thump to a bewildering rhythm, the watchers clap and sing. The observers keep to the edge of the clearing, at a respectful distance. Every now and then a dancer charges into the crowd, and the audience scrambles back in fear. The braver ones stop to throw money at the mask's feet before they flee. Farai sees the university woman rise to answer the challenge of one of the masks. She leaps at him so that the top of her head is level with his feet. She tears off the band holding together her dreadlocks and yanks up her skirt, digs her shoeless feet into the dust before him, throws her head back and shudders while he rocks at her, above her and showers himself all over her for just a minute before she ducks back to the safety of the crowd.

Applause.

The dancer pauses, then struts around searching for the next victim. His beady eyes meet Farai's and he seems to scowl through the mask. Farai feels chosen, trapped and has a weird foreboding of things to come. And now the dancer charges straight at Farai and Fatima and Enesi!

'Run!' Enesi pants, and the two girls leap back over abandoned bottles. Farai's quart tips over into the dusty, thirsty earth like an offering to unknown spirits and he freezes, cowering in the space between the two stilts. He sees the dancer sway above him and the mask staring angrily at him. The dancer leans down as if to grab him.

'Get up and run!' Fatima yells from the darkness behind. Too late, he feels the swash of the dancer's fly whisk on his back. He plunges into the crowd, ploughing up a hurried exit with his arms. Outside in the gathering dusk silhouettes scatter and he scrambles for his car, leaps in and starts the engine.

Fatima and Enesi bang on the bonnet and the windows, 'Don't leave us here! Don't leave us here.'

Deaf to their pleas, he swings across the grass towards the road.

'You're leaving us here,' Fatima cries, 'OK, go. You'll see.'

***

He bumps across the veldt. He is not very sure of his way out of the maze of dirt tracks, but a haze of city lights beckons in the east. Tree branches snap at the car windows, a wheel groans over the stump of a dead tree, a stray cow crashes away from the head-lights into the bushes. Miraculously, he finds the tarred road. A military truck roars past, horn blaring. Yellow lights flicker and vanish ahead of him.

God, he must go home and sleep.

God, he must get to warm safe home and say sorry to Veronica and find something to eat and hold her and kiss her and find some sleep.

***

The car radio switches itself on. Brenda Fassie screams:

You don't come around
To see me in the week
I'm your weekend
Weekend special

He slaps the button shut. No time for music now. Empty bottles chatter and clink on the back seat. He reaches down under his seat and fishes out a warm, fat, quart. He snaps it open with his teeth and takes a swig. For a Saturday evening, the road is fairly empty. He skirts the city centre and runs into a police road-block. He quickly slows down, squeezes the bottle between the edge of the passenger's seat and the car door and approaches the flashing

~ 10 ~

lights. An officer with reflective arm-bands beckons him to stop and steps to the side door.

'Licence please,' she says through the open window.

'I left it at home.'

'Do you have your ID?'

He extricates the ID from his purse and holds it up to her.

'Why are you driving drunk, Mr Chari?'

'I'm not drunk, Officer.'

'Now don't argue. You don't even have your seat belt on. How much have you taken?'

'Just a few pints.'

'Your car is reeking of alcohol from metres away. Do you want to kill yourself?'

Another officer, a man, armed with a gun, comes over, takes the ID from the woman officer and flashes a torch over it.

'Do you have to get drunk to write your books, Mr Chari?'

'Is it him?' The woman officer asks. 'I thought there was something familiar about his face.'

'Haven't you seen him in the papers and on TV, Sarge?'

'Well, the law makes no exception of the famous. He could lose his licence for this.'

'What are you writing now, Mr Chari?'

'Well, about ...'

'I see, you won't say. You think police officers don't read, eh? For your information, I studied one of your books for my O-Levels. What have you got in your car?'

He flashes the torch inside the car. '*Mhaiwe!* What a lot of empties, Sarge. Now, Mr Chari, give us anything you've got open.'

Farai pulls out the concealed quart and hands it to the officer. She holds it gingerly as if it were an exhibit.

'Why are you drinking so much?' she asks, as if she genuinely wants to know.

'Stress,' he chances, 'I've buried a mother and father and brother in four years and I'm having serious problems with my wife.'

'Look, brother,' intervenes her colleague, 'I'm a man like you and even if I'd lost my whole family and my wife had divorced me, it doesn't mean that I can drink and drive.'

'Why don't you go to a family counsellor?'

'We've already tried that. I'm sorry, Officer.'

'Sorry doesn't protect all the people you might injure or kill. Sorry doesn't protect you from yourself, or from car-jackers.'

'Where are you going, Farai?' asks the woman.

'Home.'

'You're not going to drink any more?'

'No.'

'How far away is home?'

'About ten k's. Look, officers. I'm drunk and I'm sorry. I'll never do it again.'

'Don't you think we should take him for a breath test, Sarge?'

'He'll fail without even opening his mouth. If he's really sorry he'll know what to do. This is Harare, man. He can't just say sorry with nothing to show for it. Give him back his ID, officer. He knows what to do.'

Farai pockets his ID. There's a pause, the three of them not knowing what to do next. Some alternatives are tricky. Then, to his disbelief, he hears himself start the car and ease off. Miraculously the officers step out of his headlights, and he's off, slipping away from the scene. He lowers his head to the dashboard, expecting to hear a burst of gunfire from behind. Nobody fires. Nobody follows him. He accelerates.

As he approaches the local shopping centre he hits the kerb with a BANG and the car swings back and loses speed. He struggles to control the vehicle, changing gear, pumping the brakes and the car squeals to a halt. He puts on the handbrake and gets out to have a look. The tyres are OK but the wheels won't turn. He gets back into the car and starts her up, but the great heap of metal won't move. Two night guards patrolling the centre offer to push and he shakes his head in despair. The problem is not with the battery or the starter motor, but with the wheels and the suspension.

He asks the guards what time they knock off and they say six in the morning. He offers them money to keep an eye on his vehicle all night and wait until he returns in the morning.

He locks the car and begins the long trudge home. The shopping centre is deserted. There are no more combis or taxis in the rank. From behind the gates and prefabricated walls dogs bark frantically as he walks past, and the ugly refrain follows on his heels. A full moon gloats over at him.

'Damn it,' he thinks, 'if I only had a cell phone I could call the car break-down company or even haul Wilbert out of bed, but no, I mustn't give him trouble, not at this time of the night, anyway.'

It's not always good to trouble your friends.

The lights in the industrial sites swell and glow, shrink and vanish and then re-emerge. They look like the headlights of approaching cars, but there is no traffic in the road. Farai takes off his glasses, wipes them on his T-shirt and peers into the dark vlei ahead of him. A bat with a faulty radar loops out of the sky and skims over his head. He falls to his knees. He sees a person in a white gown approaching him.

'Good evening.'

In the moonlight, the man's head shines bald. He is barefooted and holds a staff in one hand and a Bible in the other.

Farai takes a deep gulp of air and grunts indistinctly.

'Are you all right?'

'Yes, yes. Say, is everything all right where you are coming from?'

'Why, yes.'

'And you think I'll get home all right?'

'I don't see why not. The road is safe and there's a full moon. Besides, it's not too late. Are you going far?'

'I live straight down the road past the shopping mall, among the houses on the right. My car broke down.'

'I'm sorry about that.'

'You're a man of God, aren't you? Will you pray for me to get home?'

'Why, if you want. I started praying for you the moment I met you. I pray all the time.'

'And can you pray for my wife and children, too?'

'I'll do that too. Is something bothering you?'

'Problems at home.'

'What makes you think things are going wrong for you? You probably have a wife and children, a good job, a nice house and a car. And you have good health and life. There are many people who would envy you.'

'Do you think so?'

'Tell me, do you drink?'

'Sometimes.'

'Maybe you should try cutting down. I used to drink myself.'

'How did you stop?'

'God called me. Do you go to church?'

'I used to.'

'What made you stop?'

'I just stopped. I believe there is a God – maybe I just lost faith in churches.'

'Some churches are different. Why don't you try us? We welcome everybody. We have all night prayer meetings on Wednesday and

Saturday nights behind the mall and you are free to join us. You're a young man and you've a long life ahead of you.'

'Do you really think so?'

'Of course. But I must be on my way. I'll pray for you. Go well, and good luck with your car.'

The man of God hurries past him without turning back. His words have soothed him and given him the energy to walk faster. But Farai shudders at the thought of himself in a white gown. He does not meet any cars or people on the way. When he arrives home it is after midnight. He clicks on the remote and the electric gate shudders open. The house is in darkness and the security lights are not switched on. He waits for the gate to close, pockets the remote and approaches what feels like his grim prison for the four-thousandth time. From the other side of the fence, his neighbours' alsations give a couple of puzzled woofs. Their security lights swell, shrink, blink and turn bluish, he irritably squeezes his eyes shut against the sudden glare and then struggles with the padlocks and the lock-blocks. Inside the house all the lights are off and the alarm has not been switched on. He snaps on the lights and approaches the main bedroom. Veronica is not there. The bed is unmade, just as he had left it in the morning. He checks the children's bedrooms – they are empty too – clothes, shoes and books are strewn all over the carpets. He takes a peek into the maid's bedroom and switches on the light. She is not there. In the study he checks out the telephone. No dial tone. In the lounge the hi-fi switches itself on and off, and on and off again. He checks all the doors and windows. They are all secure.

There is no supper in the fridge and in the scullery yesterday's dishes have not been washed.

He goes back to the bedroom and throws the wardrobes open. Half of Veronica's dresses are missing.

He throws himself on the bed. Sleep, Oh sleep. He squeezes his eyelids together and messages his scalp with his fingers.

Out in the yard a car stops, engine running, and the electric gate rolls open. He hears children's voices, keys rustling, foot steps in the lounge, muted voices. Laughter. He steps out expectantly to the lounge. The lights in the lounge blink on and off and on again. There is nobody – the keys are in the door where he had left them and the children's bedrooms are empty. Her peeps through the curtains, out to the yard. The gate is closed and there is no car in the driveway.

He throws himself again on the bed and tries to sleep. He lies like that for hours, on top of the blankets. Each time he begins to fall asleep, something wakes him up.

2

A t six in the morning, when the windows are turning orange with the first fervid licks of dawn, he takes a bath. He fills the tub with hot water and soaks himself deeply before giving his body a good scrub. He shampoos his dreadlocks and then rinses them with a conditioner. Ever since he left for the States, he had decided to keep dreads, after discovering that he had left his 'afro-comb' behind. He thinks he looks well with them. Or different, anyway. He rubs himself carefully with body lotion then picks out his favourite clothes – black jeans, black cotton T-shirt, black sneakers and black socks. He even dabs himself with a little black musk.

Then he locks up. Outside the gate a woman sits in a green VW Golf, blocking his exit. It's Sunday morning, so he assumes it is one of Veronica's churchy friends but she seems anxious to talk to him.

'Are you Mr Chari?' she asks, and he nods his assent. 'We've never met. I'm Mavis Khumalo and I live in your flat.'

'Which one?'

'Oh, the one on Fourth Street.'

'Fourth Street? The two bed-roomed one? I thought there was a young man living there. An accountant.'

'The accountant left the flat to me and I've now been there for three months.'

'I was never told this. So, you've been living in my flat without my permission?'

'Your wife said it was OK for me to move in. I understood you were away, in the States.'

'I'll have to speak to her about it. I've only just got back, but I'll be here for a while.'

'Is your wife in?'

'No.'

'When I moved into the flat, I paid her the deposit and she told me she would give me the lease later.'

'So?'

'When I went to her workplace for the lease she said she was too busy to give it to me and I should wait for you to come back.'

'But I left her in charge … OK, OK, how do you want me to help you?'

'I've come for the lease.'

'Have you paid all your rent up to date?'

'Well, when I moved in I paid her the deposit but I haven't been able to raise the rent yet. You, see, I'm separated from my husband and my mother died last month and things have not been easy for me.'

Ms Khumalo is an attractive, probably well-to-do, professional but Farai finds her unapologetic manner presumptuous.

'Now listen. First you move into my flat without my permission. Then you skip rent for three months. D'you think I'm Father Christmas?'

'Things are tough for me, Mr Chari.'

'Look, I'm not new at this game. I can tell a problem tenant in two minutes. I don't care who's died or if you're divorced. Rent has to be paid, ma'am. Have you brought the money?'

She hands him a fat envelope.

He counts the notes and pockets them.

'Can you give me the lease now, Mr Chari?'

'I'm running. My car broke down last night. Call me and we'll arrange to meet later.'

'How much later? And, by the way, your phone is not working. I tried to call you all day yesterday. That's why I came to find you this morning. I don't want to keep driving over here.'

'If I had to wait three months for my rent you can afford to wait a few days for your lease, Baby.'

Farai grabs the car door and bangs it in her face. She cowers behind the window. The girl from next door – his own daughter's classmate and best friend – stands at the gate, holding a plastic garbage bag, watching them. She looks stunned. Farai doesn't even bother to say hullo, and strides angrily away to the industrial sites.

Ms Khumalo shakes her head, starts her car and drives slowly away.

***

The breakdown haulage truck is out when he arrives and he has to wait for half an hour. The security guard at the gate offers him a tin mug of tea and a bun and he politely accepts them. He sips the scalding hot tea and nibbles at the bun. Food tastes strange, like medicine that has to be taken on doctor's orders. When the haulage truck arrives they set off at once for his car.

His Mazda 323 is parked forlornly at the shops and the security men he left to guard it are nowhere to be found. He thinks perhaps they left at six when their night shift ended. The break-down man looks under the car and at the wheels and whistles under his breath.

'Is it badly damaged?'

'They'll know at the garage.'

They hook up the Mazda and drag it off to the garage. 'It's your suspension and your wheel bearings,' the break-down man tells him. 'And one of your wheels needs attention.'

'Is it serious?'

'It can be fixed but it might take a couple of days. Do you need it in a hurry?'

'Yes,' and he adds, 'I'm travelling. To sort out some things. I don't have much time on my hands.'

'It's Sunday and the garage is closed. I'll tell you what. Why don't you get the damaged wheel fixed today, so that we can work on the other problems first things tomorrow? It might speed things up. I know a place that's open today.'

Farai wheels the damaged tyre to a backyard workshop where it is soon fixed and he returns it to the garage.

'Come tomorrow morning when the mechanics are here,' the mechanic tells him.

***

He takes a combi to the city and goes to an afternoon Jazz club. The place, an open garden with chairs, tables, flowers and plenty of shade, is already full of patrons when he arrives. Waiters in khaki uniforms shuttle among the tables and the bar in the corner serving drinks and snacks. The crowd unnerves him, somehow. Voices are loud and everybody seems to be laughing. He finds a place to sit and orders a beer.

The band is taking a short break and the instruments are on the stage. The disco is playing jazz music. Oh there is Piri, the girl in Thomas Mapfumo's band. Piri holding a drink and waving at him, laughing and what ... she's coming over.

'Oh, my sweet darling, you're alone again,' Piri says.

'I didn't know you liked jazz as well,' he tells her.

'Oh yes I do,' she says, sipping her gin and tonic. She is wearing a white T-shirt, blue denim hipsters and silver slippers.

'How was the show last night?'

'The show? What show? Did you go out?'

'Don't know. I was out somewhere watching *zvigure* and my car broke down.'

'You like *zvigure*?'

'Sometimes. So how is Thomas Mapfumo these days?'

'I haven't been to a show of his in ages.'

'But I thought you were a singer and dancer in his band?'

'Me, never.'

'I must have been drunk when I met you, then.'

'You're always drunk.'

'Did you cut your dreads?'

'Ages ago. I like my hair short.'

'Really, Piri?'

'Why are you calling me that? I see you have forgotten who I am. I am Matiedza the film-maker. You did some voice dubbing for one of our videos two years ago and invited me to eat *mazondo* at kwaMereki. Afterwards we went to hear Thomas Mapfumo.'

'Oh, Mati! Of course.'

'Don't worry. It happens. Can I buy you a drink?'

'You are the first woman in months to offer me one.'

'These are not the days of roasting loincloths! After all we're not starving now, are we?'

'Of course not.'

'And we only live once.'

He talks with Mati about anything and everything, and makes her laugh. He likes her because she is almost a tomboy, and seems not to care much about what people think about her as a woman. She is an ex-combatant who has found a niche in the film world. He wonders who helped set her up. A white man, perhaps. Amazing, he thought, how many of these educated ex-combatants go out with white men. Was it because they did not paint them with the same tar and ignored the rumours of prostitution and death? Or because white men were gentle and understanding, and had money? He likes her flashing teeth and her strong dark hands and her wood, steel and brass bangles. He remembers now how she had rolled up a fat joint and persuaded him to smoke it with her in her flat before setting off with him on her scooter to the show, and how they had danced for hours on the stage. And now the jazz band is playing and the sun is warm and the drinks are cold and they are both tapping away to Hugh Masekela, Earl Klugh and Jonathan Butler. And now she's on the stage singing an old Harare Mambo tune and everybody is clapping wildly and she is back sitting on his lap and ordering more drinks. And now he is dancing on the stage with her and everyone is clapping hands and cheering till he thinks his eardrums will burst.

Eventually Mati drives him back home in her VW Beetle and drops him off at the gate of his prison and hugs him and says, 'Phone me tomorrow.'

Just as she is pulling back into the road another car, a Peugeot 406, pulls in from the other direction and turns into his driveway. For a moment he is dazed by the bright headlights and when he steps out a familiar voice calls cheerily, '*Hes*, Farai!'

'Mainini Goto!'

It's his aunt, his late mother's cousin and a much younger woman, her niece.

'Come in, come in, Mainini. Hello, Faith. What a surprise.'

As soon as the two women step out of the car he gives them each an exuberant hug.

Mainini Goto sits resplendent with middle-aged matriarchal ease while Cousin Faith, barely nineteen and decked out in purple, pierces the air in the lounge with her exotic perfumes.

'We heard you were back. We were just passing by and came to check on you. Are you all right?'

'Yes, Mainini!'

'How was the States? What did you bring us? Did you meet your cousin Lemi?'

'I talked to him on the phone.'

'Where's Veronica? Gone to church with the kids for the evening service, I suppose?'

'You know these Pentecostals. Mainini!' he says, shaking his head. ... 'Mainini!'

'What?'

'Come. Come and see.'

He leads them to the main bedroom, his bedroom, and pulls back the blankets right down to the carpet. Cousin Faith leans forward staring, as if expecting a cat or a baby viper to leap up from between the sheets.

'What is this, Mainini?' he asks, pointing to the logos printed on the sheets and the bedspread.

'That's the same material for the uniforms which the women at Veronica's company wear.'

'Logos, logos, logos, Mainini! Veronica's logos. That's what this house is all about, Mainini. This is what I have to put up with every day.'

Mainini Goto thoughtfully chews on a fingernail and leads the way out of the bedroom, back to the lounge. She looks at the logos, wondering if Farai is not becoming somewhat obsessed, after all she knows what fabric costs, and the chance of a cut-price deal ...

'I know,' she says, 'Let's talk. Maybe you can tell me tomorrow, after you have had some rest. Have you had anything to eat?'

'No.'

'You can always come to my house if you are hungry or need any-thing. Remember I am your mother.'

'All right.'

'Nobody can stop you drinking, or say drinking is bad, but you must try to cut down a bit. Veronica says you've been back three days but most of that time you've been out.'

'Did she call you?'

'Never mind. That's not why we came. We've just come to make sure you're OK. Let's talk tomorrow, when you've had some rest. Look, we have to go now or we will find Mkoma Willie waiting.'

'Is Willie still with you, Mainini? That man must have worked for decades for you now.'

'Twenty-seven years. He was eighteen when we first employed him, and he didn't even leave after your uncle died.'

Mainini is good at talking about domestic matters – gardeners, maids, loyalty, security, saving, and education. Using time wisely. A clothes designer, she believes in flowers, rockeries, beautiful driveways, gazebos and women's organisations. She would be the first to tell your gardener to climb onto the roof and sweep off the leaves, or trim the hedge. She makes you want to get on in life and be somebody she can take pride in. Somebody whose house she could drive past and boast to her church friends, 'My nephew lives here.' In this her principles intersected with those of his late father, which was why the latter, just before he died, had written her a long, prophetic letter about his children, somehow entrusting them into her care.

As Mainini drives off who should stop by but Mai Tapiwa, their neighbour. She lives two houses down the road and sometimes comes with her husband to talk, laugh and drink beers with him on an occasional Saturday evening, while Veronica sulks and sips Fanta in the kitchen. Mai Tapiwa of plum lips, long slit denim skirts and forbidden sideways eyes. Tonight she wears lipstick and eye-shadow.'I just came to check on you', she says, 'Don't worry, you'll be all OK as long as I'm here. Mai Tapiwa takes his hands in her warm manicured ones and leads him back into the house …

Mai Tapiwa has left. She came into the house and sat with him, next to him. He played her music from his collection and talked to her about himself. She asked him gently about his trip to the States. She kissed him on the lips before she left, saying her husband was waiting at the gate.

He plays jazz and traditional music. He steps out to the pantry and opens the fridge. It is nearly empty. Or is it? Did Veronica remove the food? There are two or three tiny packets of meat. He picks one of them up and examines it. The meat is red, very red, red pork and it has yellowish pockmarks like little swollen eyes, staring at him. 'Pork is bad,' Fatima had said. He hastily throws the packet down. In the pantry the shelves are bare; large, brown nauseous bugs conglomerate over little crumbs of food.

He goes into the bedroom, and plays more music on the hi-fi at the headboard. The music makes him feel expansive and he wants to hug the walls and the curtains of the bedroom but he lies still on top of the blankets, with his eyes closed. A slow inertia grips his body; he lies like that until the hi-fi switches itself to the radio. In the early morning, he vaguely hears the wake-up church service programme, Reverend Mwaita, still going strong, is preaching a sermon about faith. He is a well-known multi-denominational evangelist. Once upon a time, at the age of thirteen, Farai had attended his service in a huge tent outside the township and accepted the Lord. But his new faith, prompted by fears of hell and brimstone, had worn off in a welter of pubescent sin.

The sermon is broken by songs from the choir. Farai knows them well but when he tries to hum the tunes his voice dries up. Before the end of the sermon there is a pause, then Father Mwaita speaks again. The urgency in his voice rises to a pitch.

'Somebody out there, a child of the Lord, is having problems and he knows himself,' says Father Mwaita. 'This person is a well-meaning man but engulfed in sin. He is like an uprooted sapling

drowning in a fast-flowing river. He has lost his faith. Yes, it is you my child and I shall not say your name on the air because that would break your frail heart. You know yourself. You have not slept or eaten for days, my child. The problems you are trying to solve need a clear mind and you cannot achieve this without sleep. Why don't you try to catch a little sleep before you begin another day? Why don't you try to start afresh?'

Farai yanks the hi-fi cord out of its socket and sits up, his heart beating fast and his hands shaking. The voice injects him with a sudden energy and he staggers to the bathroom to soak himself in hot water. The sun is rising, sketching wry images of faces and figures on the bathroom walls, just like a movie. Outside, next door, the voice of a little girl laughs, and his neighbour chides his dogs.

He carefully chooses his clothes for the day, brushes his teeth, oils his locks and, deodorized, goes out and locks the house. He must go out.

***

He is late.

He marches along the path at the edge of the road. All the vehicles are going there, roaring up from behind him, very few going the other way.

The drivers of the cars and trucks and combis are stern with the importance of their mission, they don't turn to acknowledge him, or each other; only the big green truck hoots as it flies past him and the grim-faced driver raises a palm at him.

The green truck must be where the cameras and lights are.

The crew members are in the combis.

The VW Beetle that has just gone past is Matiedza's. Mati is the assistant director of the film.

Out there, two hundred metres ahead of him, weaving along the dust path at the side of the road are two people, his little daughter

Sharai and their maid Maria. Maria is holding Sharai's hand and they are walking, oh, ever so slowly down the path, towards the vlei and they must not miss the joy of the historic occasion. He must catch up with them and walk with them so that he is not alone, so that they arrive together. But where is his son, his little boy Ticha? Has he already left with Veronica?

A man with a helmet toots at him from his scooter – this must be the man doing the initial shots, capturing the footwork on Polaroid, perhaps.

The Datsun pick-up truck loaded with a mountain of cabbages, tomatoes and potatoes must be for the market scene in the script and the AFDIS truck must be bringing in the drinks already – didn't the director say there would be a party every day after the shooting?

And Maria and Sharai are moving oh, ever so slowly, floating towards the vlei. 'Maria! Sharai! Wait!'

Can they hear him? He lopes after them and now he can hear their chirruping voices and their tinkling laughter. He can see the reds, whites and greens of their clothes and their shoes. Now they have stopped for him and joyously he reaches out to grab Sharai's little hand.

'Aren't we late?' he gasps.

'Good morning Daddy,' Maria says, *'Mamuka sei?'*

Maria of peppered breakfasts and clever lunches and late lazy baths and black avocado-pear breasts, that day he burst into the children's bathroom by mistake, Maria now smiling her little, puzzled, expectant smile and saying good morning, daddy. Maria, for whom he has brought a dress and shoes to say thank you for looking after everything while I was away and now he has got her a part in the film to show the world how he lived and how he worked and what a simple, undemanding man he was …

'Can we help you, sir?'

And now he feels a searing flash in his brain and Maria shrinks to a bony, middle-aged mother with a recalcitrant brown skirt and a cheap red Sandak shoes, Sharai stretches up into a lanky, knock-kneed teenager with a schoolbag on her back and her hand wriggles awkwardly out of his grip.

'Can we help you, sir?'

***

At the garage the security man is having tea and offers him half a bun.

'Are you coming to the shooting?' Farai asks him.

The security man gives him a doubting sideways look and takes a sip from his tin mug.

'Is my car ready yet?'

'The mechanics come in at nine.'

'Tell them to work fast, because I'll need the car soon.'

There is a pub nearby, one of his favourites, and he goes there to wait. On the sidewalk the vendors are laying out their wares and he greets them jovially.

***

In The Calabash the workmen have already nailed the cables to the walls and the light bulbs are screwed on in the trees and corners. The bar has been closed for this special event. The spectators have been moved away to the shops where they have assembled and he can hear their voices shouting. Waiting for him to act. The great writer comes home.

Everything is in reverse. It has to be. And that is why the garden is empty, closed up for the show. He has to retrace every step. It must start with him at the airport leaving, his family waving from the balcony and cheering him off for the umpteenth time. It has to start with journeys into the past and forgotten beginnings. It must capture that stark moment when he spilled out of his mother's womb and screamed into a blurred world. His very first memories of faces and voices and leering shadows, of the warmth of his mother's milk dripping into his mouth, of his father towering tall and strong, naked, soapy and wet in the shower above him, with him. Of the vast little four-roomed house with innumerable nooks and insistent ghosts shivering in the bananas, and voices cackling in alien languages inside the radio. Of the sharp odour of Dorothy's bum inside the hot little rolling drum, and the salt bite of his mother's peach stick on his legs. Of hunger and crowded, stinking classrooms and toilets awash with filth, of dew in the morning on miles of grass and frivolous impossible girls. Of thorny wars between black and white, black and black, wrangles between fathers and mothers, brothers and sisters and couples who can't talk.

This will be a great big film that will include everything; a film to end all films.

***

'How long have I been like this?'

He leans back with his hands on the table and confronts his favourite barman.

'Why, Mr Chari? You've only just arrived. We let you in because you were outside and we hadn't opened. We're not open yet but we served you. That's only your first beer.'

'Give him soda water,' says a white man with one arm, a regular patron. 'I'll pay for it.'

The barmen are still cleaning the windows and lifting the chairs down from the tables. The woman at the front desk waves and winks at him.

'Have you ever been really drunk, Sir?' he asks the white man.

'Every day.'

'But why aren't you working?'

'I am working.'

'So what sort of work do you do?'

'I empty Castle bottles.'

'How much do they pay you?'

'Enough to feed my missus.'

'Are you married?'

'Yep. Got two sons about your age. Late thirties, eh.'

'And your wife loves you?'

'We tolerate each other. There comes a time in life when it's useless to fight. She doesn't hump me every day but she tries. She knows if she doesn't do that I can get me a small house any time.'

'Small house! Ha! What a dirty old man you are! Who do you think would want to have a small house with a wimp like you?'

'Anybody. White, black or blue. Small houses are not usually plastered, you see, so they don't have colours. And they are hardy as bricks. Once upon a time I fought with the missus and came here to drown me sorrows a bit. Bang I started talking with one of your soul sisters who drink here. Before I knew it I was shacking up with her in her boy's *kaya*. And she was a damn good fat mama too, cooking, washing up, ironing and all that. African women are great housekeepers. Think I must have gained two kg's in a week!'

'What did the missus do?'

'Don't know who told her, but when I didn't show up for a week she drove over in her squeaky little Datsun 120Y and beat me up with her walking stick. I don't know how, but she bundled me up onto the back seat and drove off like an ambulance. You ain't seen an angrier woman than that. I still have bruises to show for it.'

'Served you right. Are you a farmer?'

'Was. Sold me farm before you guys started all this land grabbing and turning this country into thousands of little villages.'

'So where do you live now?'

'In a little flat in town. What about you? You look like a rich black bugger with a bag full of questions and a little arithmetic in your head. Four bedroomed house with a swimming pool, probably?'

'No ways.'

'Manager or something?'

'No. I'm a writer.'

'What do you write? Newspapers? Books?'

'A little bit of everything. They are going to make a film of me.'

'Film, hey. How nice. So what brings you here? Why are you guz-zling yourself mad at nine on a Monday morning, son?'

'You wouldn't want to know.'

'Come on, boy. Out with it. Why are you so uptight?'

'I don't know where my wife is with the children and my car is at the garage.'

'Had a boxing match with your wife?'

'Came home late a couple of times.'

'You ignored her. You don't ignore a woman, boy, even if you have a small house. She probably ran off to her mother. They always run off to their mothers. You must have paid a lot of mombes, sheep and goats when you married her. Why don't you call your mother-in-law and ask her?'

'There's no phone here.'

'Here, use my cell-phone. Just don't be too long about it because my battery is nearly flat.'

Farai dials up and holds the phone to his ear. Veronica's mother answers and he says 'Makadii Mhamha?' She answers with a but-tery voice. They go through the only pleasantries possible between in-laws and, to be honest, he has never been really close to Veronica's mother. A church deacon's wife, she keeps a tight rein on her children, especially the daughters, whether they are married or unmarried, and is one of the new breed of sturdy dames trained by the harsh economic times to survive by travel-ling to neighbouring counties to buy and sell. She is hardworking and shrewd like many women married to lowly paid, unassuming

church men. He suspects she mistakes his reserve for pride or fil-
ial disrespect and that she has been fed a regular diet of untruths
about his character by her daughter. Perhaps the least salient fact
of the matter is that Farai has never forgiven Veronica the privi-
lege of having a living, seventy-year-old mother when his own
died at the tender age of fifty-three.

'Is Veronica there, Mhamha?' he cautiously asks.

'I can't say, Mwanangu.'

'Is she there or is she not, Mhamha?'

'That I can't say, Mwanangu. I can't say she is here or not here.'

'If she calls you or comes over, will you tell her I called?'

'All right, Mwanangu.'

'Any luck?' the white man asks, when he finishes talking.

'My mother-in-law won't say.'

'Probably knows but won't say. Mothers-in-law always know,
you know!'

'Can I make another call?'

'Go ahead.'

He calls Mainini Goto, his mother's cousin. 'I'm on a borrowed
cell-phone,' he tells her, 'So I'll be quick. How are you this morning, Mainini? Veronica still hasn't come back with the children. I
phoned her mother who said she doesn't know where her daugh-
er is. Do you think you know where she might be, Mainini?'

'I've no idea. Did you try her sisters, or your sister Tindo? Where
are you now?'

'I'm in a pub, talking to a friend.'

'In a pub, already? Are you all right?'

'Yes, Mainini?'

'Did you sleep?'

'A little.'

'Have you eaten?'

'A little.'

'Look, Farai, you'll have to forget about Veronica for a little while and concentrate on looking after yourself. It's time you learnt to respect and value yourself. The children are safe. Take that from me. That's all I can say. I think you and I need to talk. I wasn't happy to hear you have been harassing people who come to your house.'

'What people?'

'That woman, for instance, who came to pay rent for one of your flats. Weren't you violent? She reported the matter to the police.'

'Harassing people! Violent! Police! Who's been talking to you about this, Mainini?'

'Never mind. Why don't you come to my house this evening? You and I need to talk.'

'I have no car. I don't know if it will be ready then.'

'No car? What happened?'

'I forgot to tell you I had a little accident. Nothing serious. The car's being fixed.'

'Oh, Farai, do be careful.'

'And even if I get the car I might be busy with the shooting. They are making a film of my life.'

'A film. How wonderful!'

'Don't worry, Mainini. I'm very happy and I'm all right. I'm very, very happy and I feel great! I've never felt happier in all my life. And who knows, Mainini, I might get you a part in the film.'

'Any luck this time?' the white man asks him when he hands over the cell-phone.

Farai shakes his head. Suddenly his eyes gleam and he throws his hands in the air and laughs. 'Never mind. My aunt said my children are safe and I believe her. She's a good, good aunt and I love her. I love her and I love my wife and my children and my sisters and my brothers and my friends and anybody who wants to be loved by me. I love you, old man. Are you good at acting? Because if you are I'll give you a part in my film. Oh yes I will. Barman, can you give us another round, please?'

3

'**Y**ou can't have it today,' the mechanic straightens from under the car and wipes his brow. The morning promises to be hot. Farai pleads, 'I need it today. Isn't there somebody I can talk to?'

'The manager will tell you exactly what I have told you. You can go and talk to him if you like.'

Farai worms his way through the graveyard of mangled cars to the manager's office. Some cars are being panel-beaten, others painted and still others having their engines fixed. It is a small, crowded yard. Every possible space is taken up and the road outside is jammed with a long line of ailing vehicles. Farai nods at the two or three other mechanics at work.

In the office he cheerily greets the secretary and explains his problem to the Indian manager, who has his hand clamped around a cash box and is poring over some quotations.

'What did my mechanic say?'

'He said perhaps tomorrow, but I need it today. It's very urgent. Please …'

'It depends if we can get the parts, and there is a long queue of other cars. Monday mornings are always bad, Sir, with everybody bringing in the cars they've bashed up over the weekend. People are driving like crazy these days, you know, and some of them are drunk or going around with fake licences.'

'But my car was towed in yesterday.'

'I know.'

'It's very urgent. I need that car on the road and don't care what it costs.'

'We'll see what we can do. Come back at three o'clock.'

'Thank you , Sir,' Farai says with slight sarcasm, emphasising the 'sir'. Damn it, he thinks, in the days of Ian Douglas Smith these Indians used to squeeze us of our pennies in their wholesale shops, supermarkets and take-aways, but now with ESAP and this newfangled liberalisation creeping in they are digging up those billions stashed away in ceilings and walls and investing in garages, real estate and even banks.

Damn it. How can his car do this to him when he needs it most with all those people waiting for him. And where has Veronica gone with the children? Where is his daughter Sharai and his little boy Ticha? Will he have to go and pick them up for the shooting? If he doesn't won't they be late? And why has his sister Tindo not called him? Damn it, the home phone is dead. He thinks he remembers seeing the unpaid phone bills. What on earth was Veronica up to when he was away? Letting the accounts go do the dogs?

In the road a combi going to the city stops to drop off some commuters. On the spur of the moment he flags it and runs to catch it. The combi is full. He wriggles into half a seat near the door. The fat woman with a bag of maize on her lap refuses to budge. The *hwindi* slides the door shut and leans against the door and over him, in a position that only *hwindis* can endure. Farai reaches into his back pocket for the fare. He fishes out a note and holds it up. The *hwindi* glances at the note and nonchalantly looks away.

'What is the fare?' Farai asks the fat woman and she frowns and shifts the bag of maize to another knee. A little schoolboy going to the afternoon 'hot seat' class and with a haircut like Ticha's raises three quick fingers at him and he fishes again into his pockets, extracts a sheaf of notes, plucks two more and holds them up. The *hwindi* snatches them up, somewhat appeased.

The combi disgorges its passengers right in front of the public toilets at the western terminus. Back on his feet he pauses to check his bearings. The shock of the crowd blasts through him like speakers at a disco. A foul stink blows out from the wretched toilets. In the large sinks on the back walls of the latrines women strapped up in *zambias* rinse fist-sized tomatoes, fat carrots and rich green spinach. Tables are loaded with oranges, bananas, apples and pears. Over open gas fires enterprising vendors serve sadza, chicken, *matumbu* and *guru* to jacketed and suited young bureaucrats with bright impatient ties while municipal police look on. He almost collides with a blind man wearing dark glasses. Combis rev in rows; advancing and reversing, reversing and advancing as if it is their job to taunt the crowd and keep it in check. The touting of *hwindis* and the vendors is deafening.

He feels trapped. He steps out of the terminus and leaves the noise behind him. He ascends the new pedestrian fly-over smeared already with the slogans of the season, and steeped with the inevitable smell of human waste, past a cluster of fast-food shops, round First Street with its chic boutiques, banks and restaurants, through the Police Headquarters car park to the Customs Office, where his sister Tindo works.

He has been here several times before, so he knows his way around. He bolts up the stairs past protesting commissionaires to the offices on the top floor.

Tindo is sitting at her laptop computer, inspecting a heap of files. Her door is wide open and he marches right in.

'Mwana wamaivangu!' she yells and he grabs her from her seat and hugs her tightly.

Oh how nice to hug your mother's daughter, to hold someone you know in your arms, here, far from the maddening crowd below. Tindo is his youngest sister, the sibling he taught the ABC and 1

+ 1, and with whom he went hunting *maroro* in the vleis of their childhood. She had helped look after their mother when she died, sleeping on the same bed with her, washing her clothes, shaving her head and braving the smells of cancer. Later, after both their parents died, he had supported Tindo at university and then helped she and her husband raise money for a loan to build their own house.

'Busy as usual,' he laughs, and adds, dramatically. '*Wena uzaba uCompany Secretary! Look at you. Laptop, phone, coffee-maker, fridge. Next we'll hear you're the Acting Deputy Managing Director.'

'*Kutyei?* It's what our mom and dad wanted, isn't it? Isn't it why we spent days weeding in the rain?'

'I don't suppose you have any hot stuff around, do you?'

'No, no. We don't stock such things, and it's too early anyway. Do you want a cup of coffee, or tea?'

'*Nikisi,* Bantu. I don't want tea *hobvu inovhuna* spoon, like those *mapostori veku Gwehava. Mapostori ari nani.'**

'Is that why you are now sporting dreadlocks?'

'I forgot to pack my afro comb in my bags when I left.'

'*Hesi mhani.* So what will vanaAmbuya say?'

'Who cares?'

'You gained weight.'

'I was giving myself *chikafu che*feeding everyday. *Asi ndowako†* *we*feeding, remember?'

'Oh, Mbuya VaDhafu! Do you think she's still alive? We should go home more often to see the old folks.'

'So, how is my *mkwasha* and my little wife Nyasha?'

---

*No, people. I don't want strong tea which breaks spoons, like those Apostolic Faith worshippers at Gwehava. The Apostles who think themselves well up.
† Is it your food?

'Fine. We were planning to come and see you yesterday, after we heard you were back.'

'Now Tindo. I know you're busy and won't take up your time. Can I make a few phone calls? Your line is direct, isn't it?'

'Who do you want to phone?'

'Veronica.'

Farai dials the number. 'Premier Discount House? Can I speak to Veronica Chari? Yes, I'm holding. Oh, she's not there? You don't know where she is? You say she didn't say. And you are her new secretary? Your name is – ? Sthabile. Oh, Sthabile. Thank you, Sthabile. Please hold, Sthabile.'

Farai puts the phone behind his back and hisses at Tindo. 'I don't know where Veronica is, and her secretary doesn't either.'

'Mkoma Farai …'

'See. I've told you these things all these years and you have never believed me.'

'Mkoma Farai, please …'

'Maybe you know where she is, Tindo.'

'There you go again, Mkoma Farai. Nobody can stop you once you start.'

'Today you'll all know who I am. I'm calling her boss.'

'Mkoma Farai, not here please. And can you lower your voice? People might think we're fighting.'

'Yes, Sthabile, sorry to keep you holding. Can you give me Walter please. Walter? Walter Nzombe, your Deputy General Manager. Who will you say is speaking? Oh, just tell him it's Farai, an old friend.'

'Do you really have to do this, Mkoma Farai?'

'Yes, Sthabile, I'm holding. He's on another line, is he? Can you interrupt him? Tell him it's very urgent.'

'Mkoma Farai, stop it. You can't do that here, in my office!'

'Shut up, Tindo. I know what I'm doing! Yes, Sthabile. Am I

through now? Yes, Walter. Long time. How are you? Who am I? It's me Farai. Farai Chari. We went to University together, remember? I'm Veronica's husband. She's your assistant or something. I suppose nobody calls you Walter any more and you are now used to being called DGM Nzombe. You are all doing very well, with your company cars and company loans and all that. I see we now even have company sheets in our bedrooms. Ha, ha. Some novelty! You mean, how can you help me? Ah, yes, can you tell me where my wife is, Walter? You don't know? But you're her boss, aren't you? Did you give her a day off? You're not in a position to tell me, you say. You think it's a domestic matter between me and her, is it? Very well, Walter. Thank you very much, Walter. Have a nice day.'

'Now look what you've done, Mkoma Farai.'

'I haven't finished with them yet.'

'What are you going to do?'

'I'm going to Premier Discount House right now to find out what's happening.'

'Mkoma Farai, wait!'

He is already bounding down the stairs, down to the roaring streets.

***

'Where is she?'

The secretary at the Discount House eyes him nervously and dials two more extensions.

'Have you seen Mai Chari?' she asks another woman.

A small crowd gathers at the reception. There are two or three male messengers in blue and four women. The women are all in uniforms patterned with the company logo, the same material Veronica had used for the sheets for their bedroom. They stand in a ring, awed by his hair and unconventional style, this man who writes books and is married to one of their superiors. They whis-

~ 40 ~

per ominously, avoiding his eyes. He knows one of them, Grace, from the days when he used to pick up Veronica in his VW Golf, some twelve or so years ago when Veronica was still an assistant accountant, without a company car. Outside, on another floor, the voices of singing women rise and fade.

'Has anyone died?'

'No, no, Mr Chari,' says Grace. 'Can we give you something to drink?'

'A whisky or a gin. Do you have that?'

'No, Mr Chari.'

'So where is she?'

Grace takes his arm and walks him down a passage, away from the reception. 'Her secretary says she was in briefly this morning.'

'Show me to her new office.'

'It's down this corridor, but she's not there.'

He steps out in the indicated direction. The carpets are red and the walls made of gleaming pine wood. All the doors are labelled in large white letters: DGM. AGM. CHIEF ACCOUNTANT. CHIEF AUDITOR. A voice inside him tells him, 'No, you can't be doing this, Farai.' He turns back and walks past the reception, to the elevators.

'Mr Chari, wait.' Grace disentangles herself from the crowd and approaches him. 'I think I know where she might be. Last week she was talking of writing her institute examinations and was staying back after hours to study in her office. Don't tell her I told you this, but I think she's writing one of her final papers today.'

'But why wouldn't she want me to know that? Come on, Grace. You are a woman and you are married. Wouldn't you tell your husband if you were writing exams?'

'I would.'

'Exams. Now that makes some sense. She obviously doesn't want me to know where she's writing them, or thinks I might disturb her. But what about other things – disconnected phones, unpaid bills and tenants who are allowed to skip rents, fridges and pantries suddenly emptied?'

'Mr Chari?'

'You wouldn't understand, Grace. I left her with enough money for everything, and now this. Maybe she used all the money to pay for her exams.'

'Please, Mr Chari, remember not to let her know I ever spoke to you.'

'I won't. Thanks, Grace. You're a good friend. I've got to go. They're shooting a film of my life, and there is a part for a secretary, if you can act. I had a little accident, and must get the car and find my children. My children have to be there.'

***

He stands in the boisterous, swirling street, looking for a taxi. He sees Grace following behind him, hurrying down the pavement. When he stops to allow her to catch up with him she walks right past him with her face down. Across the street he sees Mai Tapiwa step out of a restaurant with two lunch-boxes tucked under her arm. He waves at her but she is sucked into the crowd. At the street corner he sees Fatima in her black T-shirt and purple shorts sitting on an empty crate of beer bottles, selling cotton wool pads, towels and lotions spread out on a white cloth. When he greets her and reaches out to shake her hand, she sweeps up her wares and saunters towards a half-loaded combi .

At the taxi rank his sister Tindo grabs his arm and pulls him back. 'Mkoma Farai, wait.'

'Leave me alone,' he slaps her hands off, jumps into the taxi and slams the door shut, in her face. The dozing taxi driver sits up and waits for instructions.

'Muzhanje Park,' he pants.

The taxi driver reverses out of the rank, swings back past a frantic waving Tindo and sidles into a free lane. He scratches at a large, old gash on his forehead caused by an ugly accident, or, perhaps, an attack or a fight.

On the radio, a jiti singer cries.

Ndakakupa zvese zvawaida Marita
*Asi hapana kana chawakandipawo**

'Is the music too loud?' the driver asks him.

'Leave it on,' he says. 'There is too much noise outside.'

'Women,' The taxi driver sighs, non-commitally.

He is not sure on what street Veronica's young sister Maidei lives. He only knows how to get there. The taxi reverses down the road, searching among the houses. The meter ticks on relentlessly.

'Here,' he calls out, eventually, and they stop at a small, two bed-roomed house in a walled yard. 'Wait for me. I'm coming.'

He goes in through the wire gate. Maidei comes out of the house holding a young baby. She has just given birth to her second boy and is on maternity leave. She is barefoot and in her flannel night-dress, she seems round and soft the way new mothers often are, her ample breasts bulging with milk. She has full lips and liquid eyes like Veronica's, but she is shorter and her arms are darker and marked with large veins. Her fingers are long and straight; the nails are painted purple. Farai gets on well with her, but some-times regrets not having played enough of the *chiramu* game with her before she became engaged and then married.

'Babamukuru! What a surprise. *Kwakanaka here*? When did you come back from *kuchirungu*? What did you bring us back? How arc the others at home? Aren't you coming in?'

'I'm running, Mainini Maidei. My car is at the garage and the film people are waiting for me.'

'Film people?'

---

*I gave you everything you wanted, Marita
But you never gave me anything back.

'Didn't Veronica tell you? They are making a film about my life and you'll all be in it.'

'How nice. And why is the car in the garage?'

'I had a little accident.'

'Weren't you hurt?'

'No.'

'Was the car badly damaged?'

'Not too much. They'll fix it. Is Veronica here with the children, Mainini?'

'Sisi Vero, no.'

'When did you last see her?'

'Last week, at mother's plot.'

'Well, I don't know where she is. I haven't seen her for days now.'

'What did you do to her, Babamukuru?'

'What makes you people think I'd do things to her? Do you know what she did to me and is doing to me? Are you sure she's not here?'

'How could I lie to you, Babamukuru?'

'I called *mhamha* at the plot and she said Veronica wasn't there. And now you're telling me she's not here. So who's not telling the truth?'

'Have you tried Sisi Mai Winnie's place?'

'No.'

'Maybe you should check there.'

'I'm going there right away.'

'But Babamukuru, wait. Are you going away without eating? Have you eaten?'

He jumps into the taxi and they reverse again towards the main road.'

'My *muramu*,' he tells the driver. 'She's just got married and her husband is away in Beitbridge. I helped them raise money to pay

~ 44 ~

the deposit for the house.'

'What happened to your wife?'

'It's a long story.'

***

The taxi stops again at Veronica's older sister, Mai Winnie's place, a sprawling four bedroomed house with a small, well-tended yard. The driver switches off the engine and taps suggestively at the meter.

Farai opens the gate and goes up to the kitchen door and knocks. The door opens a crack and his daughter Rumbidzai peeps out at him.

'Rumbi! What are you doing here? Why aren't you at school? Where is Maiguru Mai Winnie? Won't you let me in?'

The door swings opens and he enters. He sits on a sofa in the lounge waiting. A young woman with a maid's doek comes in and kneels on the floor to greet him. When she touches his hand her fingers feel reassuringly rough and hard.

'Where is Rumbidzai?' he asks.

'Rumbidzai is not here, Babamunini.'

'But I saw her at the door just now.'

The maid shakes her head.

'Who are you?' he demands.

'Godknows.'

'Your name is Godknows?'

'Yes.'

'Where do you know me from?'

'You came here to drop off Mainini and the children last Christmas. And I did your books at school.'

'Where is Maiguru Mai Winnie?'

'She's gone to work.'

'And Babamukuru?'

'Gone to work too. They'll be back at five.'

'Is Mai Rumbi, Mai Rumbi, my wife, here?'

'No, she's not.'

'Who's that talking in the bedrooms?'

'There's nobody in the bedrooms, Babamunini.'

'Can I look?'

He opens the children's bedrooms and looks in the built in cupboards and under the beds. He pauses at the main bedroom and tries the handle. It does not open. He squints through the keyhole.

'They always lock the main bedroom when they go out,' says Godknows.

'Are you sure my children are not here?'

'Yes.'

'When did you last see them?'

'Last week, at *mbuya's* plot.'

'OK. I'm going.'

'Shall I give you something to drink?'

'No.'

'What shall I tell *mhamha* when she comes back?'

'Tell her I was here. Just tell her I was here.'

He goes back to the taxi. Godknows watches him from the French doors.

'They're not here,' he tells the driver.

'Your Maiguru's place?'

'Yes. I helped her buy the house, too.'

'You've helped your in-laws a great deal.'

' Helped my family too.'

'Way to go. You'll always be blessed.'

'Now there's only one place left to check.'

'Where's that?'

'My children's school.'

'You want to go there now?' The taxi driver taps at the ticking meter and shrugs.

'Take me there.'

***

On the way to school, they check the car at the garage.

'It's not ready yet,' says the mechanic. We've fixed the problem with your suspension. We sent your plates in for lining and are expecting them tomorrow. Try tomorrow afternoon.'

***

It's twelve-noon and his children break off at one. In the car-park the vendors are already waiting to assault the kids with their packets of popcorn, sweets, biscuits and freezits. The ice-cream man waits patiently, bantering with the housemaids from the neighbourhood who have come to fetch the little ones from school. In the yard the juniors are having assembly and the infants are playing in the hockey fields.

Farai glares at the taxi meter, then reluctantly pays the taxi driver and wanders in through the gate towards the assembly. The juniors stand in wobbling rows, singing the national anthem. The choir mistress is at the front, conducting the singing. The song is finishing and the deputy headmaster is getting ready to wind up the assembly. The teachers are standing at the front. He knows most of them by name – Rumbi did all her primary school here and now Sharai is in third grade and Ticha in his first. The teachers turn to whisper at him, to greet him.

'Hello, Mr Chari.'

'*Mabva nekupi* Va Chari?'

'When did you come back, Mr Chari?'

'Are you Bob Marley now, Mr Chari?'

'How's the writing going, Mr Chari? Any new books lately?'

'You want your daughter Sharai? I'm her class teacher and go to church with your wife, remember. Is everything OK at home, Mr

~ 47 ~

Chari?'

'We have to go now,' says Farai. 'It's urgent.' He scans the rows of girls for his daughter. The girls all look alike, in their crisp brown uniforms. The children are beginning to disperse.

'Have you seen Sharai, Emily?'

'Tariro, were you with Sharai?'

'Tryphin, go and look for Sharai in the art-room.'

'Where is Sharai? Was she here at assembly?'

Suddenly Sharai melts out from behind the classroom block, rubbing her nose and adjusting her bag. He strides over to her and puts his hand on her shoulder.

'Where were you? We've got to go. Where's Ticha?'

'Ticha is playing on the hockey fields, Mr Chari. Come, I'll show you to him. Oh, there he is.'

Ticha extricates himself from his friends, rubs his eyes, pulls up his oversized shorts and dutifully places his hand in his father's. Suddenly the hockey fields erupt into wild childish screams and cheers. Children whoop around Farai, clambering onto his knees and tugging at his waist. He acknowledges the applause with a wide grin. At the classroom block the children turn back and flee to the fields.

At the classroom block Sharai is waiting, adjusting her school bag on her back.

'All right now, Mr Chari?' her class teacher says.

Clutching a hot, tiny hand in each palm, he triumphantly leads his babies to the gate.

***

In the car park he plies them with popcorn and sweets. Parents have begun arriving to pick up their children.

'Where did you sleep last night, and the night before?' he asks.

'At Gogo's plot,' Ticha replies.

'And was *mhamha* with you?'

'Yes.'

'Did you take Sisi Maria with you?'

'Yes.'

'And *mhamha* dropped you here this morning?'

'Yes.'

'What time did she say she would pick you up?'

'We don't know.'

Damn it. He has paid off the taxi-driver and now what to do? Walk the children home, maybe. It's not too far, and there is a short cut across the clearing, behind the houses.

A white BMW drives into the car park and an old schoolmate, Simbisai, shouts at him, 'Mr Ajali!'

'Mrs Ajali!' he shouts back.

He and Simbisai were in the same A-level class, doing the same subjects and he used to go to her room at the weekends so that she could braid his hair.

'Mrs Ajali,' he steps forward and hugs her through the open window.

'How is Mr Johnson?'

Mr Ajali and Mr Johnson are characters from a literature set text they studied together. Farai knows Simbisai's husband Sam and sometimes drinks with him. Their children are in the same classes, and on the last Open Night he and Veronica, Sam and Simbisai ate and talked and danced together, when Veronica was in one of her rare, liberal moods. That night Farai and Sam cleaned out a full crate of beers and the women drove them home in a jovial escort. Simbisai is a sweet mother and wife and also now a financial director in a food company.

'Come to pick up the kids?'

'Yes, Mrs Ajali. See how old we are getting. Once upon a time we were young and handsome and beautiful.'

'We can always start afresh. Are you a Rastaman now?'

'I was out for a while and I'm going back.'

'*Zvako*. Some of us were born to slave away in offices all our lives.'

'But where is your car, Mr Ajali?'

'It's at a garage. I had a little accident.'

'Is everything all right at home?'

'You won't believe it, but I don't know where Mai Rumbi is.'

'What's wrong now, Mr Ajali? Have you been beating her up again?'

Farai leans through the window and pours everything out to Simbisai. He feels severely wronged and is longing for someone to hear him out. He tells her about his missing wife and the unpaid bills, about uncooked suppers and a fridge without food, about disconnected phones and uncollected rents. About secret exams and his wife's new church.

'That woman is killing herself competing with me,' he fumes. 'I make three times what she makes and take care of most things at home but she won't give me or herself any rest. She doesn't know what the word 'gratitude' means.'

'Maybe you've been too hard on her, Mr Ajali. Every woman wants to love her husband and children, and be a good wife and mother. There must be something you did to her. Remember money is not everything a woman needs, especially the educated, professional types. Maybe she's asserting her independence, after years of docility. You ask my husband about that. We went through that phase. Maybe she's showing you that she can be her-self even when you're away for a year.'

'But then I should come back to an efficient household, at least.'

'Give her time. Have you talked to your in-laws about it?'

'They all take me for granted and gang up on me. Her mother is covering up for her crimes.'

'Why don't you talk to her aunt?'

'She doesn't have an aunt. Not the old kind anyway.'

'So where are you taking the children?'

He has not thought about that. 'Home, I suppose.'

'Do you want a ride? If your car is not ready yet it's no use cling-ing to the children. Take them back to your mother-in-law and speak nicely to her. No ranting and raving, Mr Ajali. And sit ten metres away from her so that she doesn't smell your breath. Maybe you won't even have to say anything, you know. Silence beats everything.'

'What if I take my children to my sister's place?'

'You could do that but you still have to talk to your wife's parents, eventually. Look. My kids will be here soon. Why don't I drop them off and leave you and your kids in the city on my way to work? Then you can decide where you want to go.'

A blinding flash of pain sears through his head and he leans for support on the door of Simbisai's car.

A blue Corolla moves slowly out of the pine trees towards the car-park, followed closely by a silver Cronos.

'There they are, Simbi!' he yells. 'They've come for the children!'

Spotted, the two cars reverse into the main road and turn into the suburb. Simbisai starts the BMW, rams it into gear and follows them. The silver Cronos turns into a drive and Simbi tracks it closely, losing the blue Corolla. The Cronos turns into another drive. Houses and streets fly past in a grey blur. The BMW edges closer to the Cronos and nudges it on the fender so that it skims to the middle of the road and accelerates until it is just a dot in the distance.

Farai clings to the door of the BMW and pants. The air is sour with burning rubber and petrol fumes and the four children sit frozen on the back seat.

'Are you all right?' Simbisai asks, adjusting her seat and driving mirror. 'Jump in. I think you had better go and see your sister.'

***

Simbisai drops them off near the taxi rank. The bustle of people and traffic swirl again in his ears and his eyes hurt. He clears his smudged lenses with the tail of his shirt and marches his children to the rank. People avoid him, spinning in a vortex, out of his path. They take one quick look in his direction and turn their faces away. An old woman spits hard at his feet and staggers off, in reverse motion.

At the rank a taxi toots at him and a strange familiar voices says to him, 'Where to this time?' A strange familiar face smiles and the taxi-man winds down the window and opens the back door.

'Pine Trees,' Sharai replies instinctively, taking charge. He peers into the taxi then climbs in after Sharai. He sits between the two children, holding their hands in his, not letting go.

'So you found your children.'

'Yes. Did you hear the news?'

'No.'

'The accident. Is he dead?'

'Who?'

'The man in the silver Cronos. He was stealing money from the company and getting my wife into trouble. He came with her to grab the children, my children. We chased after him in my friend's car and he went pfff, in a puff of smoke.'

Sharai points out the road to the taxi-driver. She speaks in precocious monosyllables. Farai cannot tell where they are. He has never been good at directions, anyway. Many a time, on clear nights he has driven past the gate of his own house. He is amazed at Sharai's confidence and has no clue where they're going but is glad to be going somewhere, away from the crowd. They drive for some time; then reverse into a close.

'Here. Turn here,' says Sharai.

Suddenly they are stopping in front of his sister Tindo's house and Tindo's maid Mai Chenai runs out of the house to welcome them.

Farai reads the meter, pays the driver and follows his children into the house, which is actually a small cottage. His sister is only just starting out in life. Mai Chenai kneels in front of him to do her how-are-yous and brings him an orange drink on a tray. Nyasha, Tindo's three-year-old daughter, just back from crèche, rushes in to hug them.

Farai sits on the sofa, listening eagerly to the radio. There is no news but the daily afternoon greetings programme accompanied by music. He goes out to inspect the garden. There are pumpkin vines everywhere and he thinks maybe when Tindo comes he will ask her to prepare him his favourite vegetable – pumpkin leaves in peanut-butter sauce.

'*Futi futi* you don't have pumpkin leaves like ours in your garden, Ticha,' Nyasha says.

'*Futi futi* you don't have a swimming pool like ours,' his son laughs back.

'*Futi futi* you don't go to crèche like me.'

'*Futi futi* you can't write your name.'

'*Futi futi* I can count up to one hundred.'

Farai follows the children into the house. Outside a cloud rolls over the sun and in the half light a blue car rolls slowly through the gate.

'It's the Corolla! Quick, quick, into the toilet, everyone! He bundles up the three children into the toilet and bolts the door. Outside a car door opens and there is a knock on the door. Sharai climbs onto the edge of the bath to look outside. He drags her down and slaps her in the face and she falls, with a muffled cry. The car starts and purrs away down the driveway. He looks through the window and then opens the toilet door.

***

---

* Hullo, my mother's child.

~ 53 ~

At eight o'clock, Tindo comes back from work late, accompanied by her husband Shepherd. Farai leaps up to hug her, crying, '*Hes,mwana wamai vangu,*'* then says to Shepherd, 'Do you want a hug, too?' and Shepherd laughs back and says, 'If there are any left.' Shepherd has two beers under his arm and he opens him one.

'*Futi futi* you don't know where my daddy goes every day after work,' Nyasha starts.

'Where's that?' Sharai asks.

'*Futi futi* my daddy goes to his own church with other men.'

'What does your daddy do at his church?' Farai laughs.

'He stands around the fire with the other men, even when it's hot, and then brings back two bottles of beer.'

'But don't they sing and pray?'

'They sing a lot but they never pray. *Futi futi* my father is a major at that church.'

'All right, Nyasha,' says Shepherd, 'Why don't you show them what you do at crèche?'

Nyasha sketches a dance, recites a poem, and then chants a praise poem of her totem.

Farai cheers her on and says, 'Teach Sharai and Ticha. All they know is how to sing church songs.' He opens the curtains on the French doors and sits sipping his beer straight from the bottle. It smells like urine. Every now and then he glances towards the darkened driveway outside. When he goes to the toilet he tells Ticha to keep watch.

Tindo and the maid bring in supper; sadza and cabbage and tiny pieces of meat.

'*Futi futi* we eat sadza, cabbage and meat most days.'

'Nyasha, we don't eat and talk at the same time, do we?' Tindo says mock severely.

'Hullo, my mother's child!'

Farai plays with his fingers and tries a little cabbage.

'But aren't you hungry?' Tindo asks him, tipping a little more meat onto his plate.

'Mhamha, *futi futi* Sekuru Baba Rumbi must dye his hair with shoe polish, just like Sekuru Mhaka. And he must get wipers for his glasses. And Mbuya too has glasses. Sekuru Maglasses, Mbuya Maglasses. I wonder if they take them off when they go to bed.'

Farai puts down his plate and goes to the toilet. He feels empty, weightless, lost. He squats over the funnelled hole, trying to empty himself of nothing. There are no toilet rolls, just a newspaper crushed between the piping and the wall. He tears off a page of the paper and something catches his eye. He excitedly buckles his trousers and bursts into the lounge, clutching the newspaper.

'Look at this,' he says, ' I told you, Tindo, didn't I?'

'What is it?' Tindo wipes her plate with sad resignation and looks up.

'Look at this. CORRUPTION EXPOSED AT DISCOUNT HOUSE. I told you, Tindo. Don't you see? Look at this picture. It's him, don't you see? He's been corrupt for years and they never knew it. Stealing right under their noses and pushing all the blame on Veronica. She's just a poor victim of their system. I've told her many times to quit and work for me but she won't hear of it. Her eyes are set on promotion, on him. She was following him, coming with him to steal my children and look what's happened.'

'We can talk about this tomorrow,' says Tindo, picking up the plates. We'd better get some sleep. Some of us have a long day tomorrow.'

'But Tindo, why do you always want to cut me off?'

'Because you only want to listen to yourself.'

Shepherd coughs and picks up the empty beer bottles. Mai Chenai kneels to announce that the spare bedroom is ready.

'Let me show you where you'll sleep,' says Tindo.

'I'm sleeping here in the lounge with the children.'

'Why?'

'So that I can look out for the blue Corolla. I want the children here on the carpet with me. That goes for Nyasha too.'

'Nyasha wets the bed and wakes up frequently at night. She would disturb you.'

'I'll sleep on the floor with Sharai and Ticha, then.'

'All right. You have it your way. It's just that when you visit other people's houses you should learn to respect your hosts.'

Tindo moves the sofas and spreads out the blankets, sheets and pillows. She hauls the sleeping Sharai and Ticha into the sheets and covers them up.

'Good night, then,' Tindo says, closing the curtains. Shepherd is already in his pyjamas, smiling and saying, 'Sleep well, *tsano*.'

Farai switches off the light and slips between the sheets next to his two babies. They are both already deeply asleep, snug in their vests and underwear. He puts an arm over them. Outside at the neighbouring house he hears the voice of Thomas Mapfumo rising and receding and voices talking in the night.

'Baba Nyasha,' he calls out softly.

'Yes, *tsano*.'

'Is there a shebeen at the house next door?'

'Why, *tsano*?'

'They are playing Thomas Mapfumo's music.'

'Maybe it's their hi-fi.'

'Baba Nyasha,' he calls again. 'I am just thinking … Now that there is nothing here for me, maybe I can take the children with me when I return to the States. I could live and work there, and send for all the children, Nyasha, too, as well as all my other nephews and nieces. They could all have a good education. The school fees would not be a problem.'

'We'll talk about that tomorrow, *tsano*.'

A car screeches down the road outside. He rises and opens the curtains. There is nothing to be seen except darkness. He lies down and gently pulls the blankets over the two little bodies. Their cheeks are warm to his fingers and their breath moist.

***

Once upon a time in our dew in the morning days when I was a baby and you must have been fifteen you used to hitch me up on your shoulders and I wet your neck with my little bum. You took me to the vlei and found me maroro *and taught me the names of fruits, flowers and birds. From boarding school you mailed me biscuits that arrived pitifully crushed to powder in envelopes colourfully inscribed 'Hi Tindo!' You taught me to read, write and sing. Mother often said 'Farai and Tindo love each other,' but I was too young to understand. We were poor but very happy. We had our family lingo, our own codes of humour. In the evenings we would gather together over steaming mugs of coffee to chat and gossip. But that was back then and now I have grown up. Now you take my children – your nieces – for regular outings and you tell them fantastic tales about our family. You are our griot.*

But things have changed and I can somehow see through you. You are no longer the giant you seemed to be when I was little. How now, Mr Know-it-All? Where to now, Mr All-in-Charge? So you want to sleep with your babies in your arms forever and in my house too? Or take them back with you to the glorious States, take all our children with you, Mr Do-it-All? What makes you think we would want you to take our children with you, Sir? You are a caring, generous and intelligent man, my dear brother, but sometimes you miss the little points. Can't you guess, for instance, that I have been in touch with Veronica since you started falling apart, that I've been keeping her fully briefed and even trying to patch things up between you two? Can't you see what your three sisters, Kata, Bertha and myself are doing behind the scenes? Don't you realise what your behaviour is doing to everybody in the family, all the stress and anxiety your are causing us? What if you drink yourself to death? What if you get involved in a fatal accident? What if your marriage breaks up? You embarrassed me in my office, in front of my workmates; you embarrassed your wife and her boss. You are the most successful member of our family and when you speak everybody listens, but I think you in turn ought to listen to others, my dear brother. You ought to learn to relinquish authority, to delegate more ...

4

At five in the morning Tindo wakes the children up to give them a bath.

'Did you get any sleep?' she asks him, optimistically.

'A few hours,' he lies.

'Good.'

He gets up and sits on the sofa so that the maid can clear the bedding and clean up the lounge. Radio Zimbabwe is already on. The early morning church service programme is over; he has just missed it. Now there is a fast-paced musical show hosted by one of the country's veteran broadcasters. He's one of the kind of well-meaning but old-fashioned DJs used to hectoring their audiences and plying them with truisms. Today his voice is charged with an infectious zeal that promises something more in the offing.

Tindo gets the children dressed and fed, fed as only children can be at six in the morning, bungling with their schoolbags, socks and plates of porridge in other people's houses.

'I'm taking Sharai and Ticha to school,' Tindo announces.

'How?'

'How else? With the combis of course. That's how we people get around here.'

'And how will they get back?'

'Don't worry. I've already arranged for that. My ATM card is not working and I'm a bit short of cash. Can you spare me some money for their combis and for their lunches? We do our groceries once a month.'

Farai digs into his pockets and hands her a couple of notes.

'Sisi Mai Chenai will fix your breakfast later and Shepherd will be around for you. He's not going to work. What are your plans for the day?'

'I must go home and make sure everything is all right, then go to the garage and check on the car.'

'Maybe you don't need the car right now.'

'Oh, yes, I do.'

'And after that?'

'I have to check the car, get the phone reconnected, go through the mail, see some people about my visa ...'

'All right, but don't you think you should see a doctor?'

'I'd rather go to the pharmacy.'

'My supervisor at work says she knows someone who might be able to help you.'

'A doctor?'

'No, just somebody.'

'I'm all right. I feel fine. I'll sleep it off.'

'Well, if you say so. Because you're older than me, I can't argue, can I? Call me if you need anything. And please, Mkoma Farai, no drinking.'

'Sure.'

He watches her leaving with the three children and feels that he'll be all right. He takes a cold shower in the toilet, which doubles as the bathroom, and dries himself with his T-shirt; there is a small damp towel on the rail. He asks Mai Chenai for toothpaste, squeezes a blob onto his palm and rinses his mouth with a finger.

He dabs some Vaseline on his face and shakes his locks into place. Mai Chenai brings him a mug of tea with two slices of buttered bread and places them on a side table in front of him. Shepherd comes briefly out of the bedroom, in his pyjamas, to use the toilet, smiles at him and says 'Good morning, *tsano*,' before asking if he has slept well.

Mai Chenai sits on the sofa in front of the French door and watches him eat. He takes slow, deliberate sips and nibbles at the bread. He wonders why she is sitting with him, watching him, and why she is not in the kitchen, washing up dishes or scrubbing floors. Perhaps she has done that already, waking up at four o'clock, the way most domestics do. She is an excellent maid and has been with Tindo from the day Nyasha was born. Almost Tindo's age, he remembers that she has two children older than Nyasha and is divorced; that the new man she tried to live with is in prison for raping her oldest daughter; and that she has had to send her children to her mother in the countryside, so that she can look after another woman's household. Now here she sits, politely fingering the edges of her jersey, the frayed edges of her life, sitting quietly as if somebody has planted her before him, to keep him company. He wants to talk to her, ask her where she was born and what school she went to and how her daughter is doing with her mother; find out if her child has recovered from the unspeakable act perpetrated on her by a ghastly man. But conversation across classes is not easy, or so people think.

She sits there listening to the radio with him, and he knows she knows most of the songs by heart, that if she was alone she would be humming to herself or singing with the radio.

Ndati bhutsu yangu yapera
Ndichifamba ndichitsvaka ndichitambudzikira iwe*
Uchanditsvaka

---

*I say the heels of my shoes have worn off
From walking and searching and worrying about you

Uchandishaya*

The DJ is growing more excited. His anecdotes are disjointed though the insinuation in the music is becoming more pointed. He is talking about an old man without a name. An old man whom the whole world knows is on the verge of death.

'And this old vatezvara *chews up a young man's lobola. He munches all the cattle, sheep and goats and gobbles up his fortune,' the DJ says, 'And the vatezvara proudly goes to the Growth Point every day in the smart suits, ties, scarves, shoes, and hats that his* mkwasha *bought him. And the vatezvara gives his equally elegant wife half the fortune given him by the young man, so that she can go south to shop for things to sell, and increase their worth tenfold. This young man buys a house and has three children with his wife. Then one fine morning the old vatezvara wakes up and tells his young* mkwasha, *'I'm taking back my daughter. You are not worthy of her!*

'Is that the way to go, folks? I say folks, is that the way to go? And if you were that young man, folks, what would you do? But as our good brother, Ray Phiri from south, said:

You can't spend your life just taking,

You can't spend your life just taking.'

'Where is Baba Nyasha?' Farai asks, suddenly, urgently. Mai Chenai knocks on the bedroom door and Shepherd comes out in an unbuttoned shirts and jeans.

'Can we go now, *mkwasha*?' Farai says.

'Just a minute. Give me a cup of tea, Mai Chenai, but no bread.'

***

'The people next door were playing Thomas Mapfumo all night,' Farai tells Shepherd as they walk to shops. 'Do they always do that?'

---

*You'll look for me
You won't find me

'Sometimes.'

They get into a combi and Shepherd pays for them both. The driver is playing a Harare Mambos tape at full blast. Virginia Jangano sings imploringly:

Amainini handei kumusha

*Hupenyu hwemudhorobha hunoshusha**

They get off at the western terminus and the noise of the crowd assaults him again. He covers his ears with his hands and follows Shepherd into another combi. At the shops the vehicle stops to pick up some passengers and an army truck loaded with soldiers roars past through a red traffic light and all the soldiers look away from the combi, away from *him*.

'Do you think Rumbi should know about this?' Farai asks.

'There's nothing she needs to know about, *tsano*,' Shepherd says.

***

They find the house deserted. A couple of letters lie on the bar, inside the gazebo. Their gardener Thomas is nowhere to be found. Farai opens the letters at once. There is a cheque from the US Internal Revenue Service for his tax refund, a letter from a fan, a belated reminder from the telephone company asking him to settle an unpaid bill, a magazine, and the final page proofs of his latest book from a local publisher. He tries to open the French door in the veranda but strangely one of the two padlocks won't open. Perhaps Veronica has changed the locks in his absence, and forgotten to tell him.

He decides to call a locksmith from Mai Jane's house next door. He jumps over the fence while the gardener there holds back the alsations (during the day the dogs are more manageable). Mai Jane shows him the phone and the directory and withdraws to the kitchen to give him privacy. He calls a number in the yellow pages

---

*Co-wife let's go to the rural areas
City life is a headache

and thanks Mai Jane. As he walks back towards the fence he hears Mai Jane say to her maid, 'Have you heard about Baba Rumbi …?'

The key-cutter arrives on a scooter in twenty minutes and makes quick work of the lock, pockets his fee and leaves. The air in the house is stuffy and Farai opens the curtains and the windows in the lounge.

'I've no drink to offer you, unfortunately,' he chuckles says to Shepherd, in the half gloom. 'You know this house is a nunnery.'

Together they replace the burnt-out bulbs on the veranda and at the front door. 'Damn it. I forgot to phone the garage about the car.'

'You can check them this afternoon.'

Shepherd reads a magazine while he leafs through the page proofs. 'Got to read these and send them back by Friday.' It is good to have things lined up for his attention, to keep him busy. 'Well, I won't keep you any longer, *mkwasha*. You can go.'

'What will you eat, *tsano*?'

'I'm not hungry.'

'There's a take-away restaurant near the garage. If you need anything you can lock up and come over to our house. I'll check on you this evening, or tomorrow.'

***

He sits at his desk in the study, poring over the proofs. The book, a collection of short stories, had kept him busy for some months before he left for the USA. He had worked at it solidly, sometimes going to bed at three in the morning. And now here was the collection, finished and edited, waiting for his final approval, and before it was launched before the eyes of the world.

He reads through the first story and begins to doubt himself. He is tired and the words are swimming on the page and he wants his car back and he has to decide about the children and the film project has been postponed. The proofs are delicate work and he'll have to do them later.

He changes his clothes, closes the curtains and windows and takes a combi to the garage to find out about his car.

'It's nearly ready,' the manager tells him, 'But you will have to pay a seventy-five per cent cash deposit for us to complete it.'

'You sharks! You never told me about the deposit!'

'Didn't we? Didn't my secretary tell you?'

'It's not on the invoice.'

'It doesn't have to be on the invoice. That's how we operate here, with new customers. Take it or leave it. Are you paying the deposit, Sir?'

'I'm going to get the police!'

'Suit yourself. … Matthew!'

Mathew, the mechanic, walks in like a robot.

'Take out the bearings, Matthew.'

Matthew jacks up the car. Farai grabs at some invoices on the desk and flings them in the manager's face, then slams the door and strides out of the yard towards the road. Behind him somebody whistles, but he strides on, automatically flagging the combis coming up behind. He marches down the road, looking straight ahead, but not one of the cars stop for him. Then he runs. He runs along the road till the sweat pours off him, right down to the police station at the shops.

At the station there is a young corporal sitting at the counter. Farai leans towards him, panting, wiping his face with the collar of his shirt.

'Can I help you, Sir?'

He explains his problem but before he is half way through the young man stops him and asks for his name. 'Are you Mr Farai Chari? I think I know your story. Somebody has just phoned about you. The manager at Bottit garage. He says you were violent and caused havoc at his place.'

A woman officer steps in from a side room and eyes him suspiciously.

'This is the man the manager at the garage phoned about, Sarge.'

'I know him. We've already met,' says the officer. 'Hello, Mr Chari. You love the police, don't you? Remember me? We met at a roadblock two or three night ago when you were driving drunk. You slipped through before we'd finished with you. My colleague was going to fire at you but I stopped him, because we know you.'

'Is he the Chari who writes books?'

'Yes, imagine.'

'I studied his books for 'O-level.'

'Me too.'

'Funny, there's another case on him here from the public relations department,' says the corporal. 'A woman living in his flat claims she gave him rent money but he has not given her a lease, and that he molested her at his house.'

'Have they done up the docket yet?' the woman asks.

'I don't think so.'

'Now, Mr Chari, you have three cases to answer. I'm going to have to lock you up. Take him in, Corporal.'

'Why is a respectable man like you behaving like this, Mr Chari?'

Farai does not answer. He leans over the counter holding his face in his hands.

'He says he has problems at home.'

'But we all have problems at home. Mr Chari.'

'Corporal, did he beat up anyone or damage property?'

'He banged doors and threw papers.'

'Then there's no GBH. The rent case is really a public relations matter. We might have problems with that. Get him out of here, Corporal. If he makes another wrong move I will definitely lock him up myself.'

At the building society, he signs a withdrawal slip and fills in a figure. He does not bother with the date, which he cannot remember, or his address. Anyway, the girl at the counter knows him and usually jokes with him. Now she smiles gloriously, completes his slip, and counts him out his money without even asking for his ID. He plucks out a note from the sheaf she gave him and hands it to her and she claps her hands, smiles, and waves at him as he turns to go.

He marches back to the garage, not bothering with the combis. They drive past him, back and forth, back and forth. Coming and going, coming and going, reversing and advancing. One of them shoots up from behind him and he sees Shepherd with his head out of the window, whistling and jabbing ahead with a Caps United flag. He hurries on.

At the garage, the manager looks at his money spread out on the counter and says, 'But we have already taken out your bearings. You reported the matter to the police, didn't you? Why do you trust them? Do you think those buggers can help you?'

Farai sits on the chair and looks out of the window. His head is hurting and he does not want to argue. On the secretary's little radio Tina Turner croons:

I don't want to fight no more.

The manager glances once at him, glances twice, glances at the pile of money on the counter and a moist brown film flashes in his eyes and he says to his secretary, 'Give him a receipt, Marjory.'

Then he turns to Farai and says, 'The mechanic is already busy with another car. He will do yours first thing in the morning. Just bring the rest of the money tomorrow and you can have your vehicle.'

***

In The Calabash his favourite waiter serves him a bottle of Black

Label, a glass of iced water and a small plate of fresh chips. He sips the water and listens to Thomas Mapfumo from the disco inside:

Joyce hauende mhaiwe
Joyce hauende mhaiwe
Mhaiwe doro renyu rinonaka
Dai waive mufushwa ndaiisa muhomwe*.

A woman with a shaved head, a tiny skirt and a plastic bag full of books comes over and joins him. He orders her a beer and offers her the plate of chips.

'You are very quiet today,' she says to him, digging in her bag for cigarettes. He has seen her here sometimes but can't remember her name.

He wipes his glasses with his shirt and looks away.

'Your rasta hair looks good on you,' she says again but he does not answer.

'You're a very lonely man. I've watched you. You don't bother anybody. You're a very nice man but people don't understand you and say bad things about you. Some people think you are reckless but you always take precautions. Come with me to my room and I will make you happy.'

He looks past her, at the coloured light bulbs in the trees.

'I won't charge you anything. I just want to make you happy, to make you talk and laugh. It pains my heart to see you so unhappy.'

She smokes relentlessly and when she uncrosses her legs he catches a glimpse of her black underwear.

'Maybe you want another woman. You want me to get you a nice

---

*Joyce, you're not going anywhere
Joyce, you're not going anywhere
Oh mother your brew is so sweet
If it was dried vegetables, I'd fill up my pockets

~ 68 ~

woman who understands? You want us to go as a threesome?'

He looks at his watch, at the setting sun, and empties his glass.

'Everybody has problems,' she says. 'Everybody needs somebody.'

He calls over the waiter and orders her a beer, and two take-away quarts for himself.

'Are you going already?'

He picks up the two quarts and clatters down the steps to the gate.

'Wait!' she calls out. 'If you need me I'll be here.'

He is walking away already, to the road and the combis. He doesn't turn back.

***

When he gets home he switches on the radio and tunes in to Radio Zimbabwe. There is a farmers' programme being aired, so he quickly switches to the turntable to play his favourite LPs. He sits slumped by himself for hours, listening to the music, only getting up to change the discs. Later he turns the radio on for the ten o'clock news, but the sound crackles and the radio switches itself off. He goes to the kitchen and fetches two sharp knives. Then leaving through the French doors, he locks up behind him and jumps over the low fence into his neighbour, Baba Jane's, yard. The alsations spot him and stand in the security light, growling. He walks straight towards them wielding the knives and they back off quealing with puzzlement.

He knocks on the kitchen door and listens for movements. He knocks again and a curtain moves and flutters. The door opens and Baba Jane's face appears, in the dark.

'Good evening. Is that Baba Rumbi?'

'Good evening, Baba Jane.' Too late, he drops the knives on the grass at his feet. 'It's all right. It's only me. Can I come in?'

Baba Jane leads him to the lounge and shows him a seat at the table, and he perches himself on a chair at the far end of the room.

'Is everything all right, Baba Rumbi?'

'Yes, yes.'

Baba Jane's balding head gleams in the poorly lit lounge. He is a retired assistant police commissioner in his early fifties; a reticent neighbour whose primary responsiblity is to his extended family. He probably has a gun locked up in a cupboard in his bedroom, for security.

'Did you hear the news?' Farai says. He does not know how to begin.

'What news?'

'The accident yesterday. That man who died in the silver Cronos. He was Mai Rumbi's boss and the police were after him. It was on the news.'

'Maybe my wife heard it. I was at work all day.'

Farai feels he is saying too much, that he must hold back. 'It's a long story.'

'Maybe I can help?'

'Anyway, my wife is in trouble, Baba Jane, and I don't know how to help her. She is on the run from the police and I've had to take the children. Now the police are after me too. And there have been all these messages on Radio Zimbabwe. You were in the police, weren't you? Can you call the police commissioner for me so that I can explain to him what's happening?'

'What do you want to tell the police commissioner?'

'It's confidential. It's something I can talk about only to him.'

'Isn't this something that can wait till tomorrow?'

'It's urgent.'

'I think you'd better call him yourself. The directory is there under the phone.'

Farai looks up a number and dials it. A male voice answers after a while, asks for his name and his address and listens as he struggles to narrate his problem.

'It's very, very urgent. I have something important to tell the police. Please come at once.'

He hangs up. The two men sit in the lounge without talking. He has been here before, first when he came to give his condolences after Baba Jane's brother died, sliced up by a giant lathe in a mysterious, work-related accident, and second when Baba Jane invited him to join a men's fellowship church meeting at his house. They sit silently together for half an hour perhaps, until a car stops at the gate and hoots.

'It's the police!' says Farai. He hurries out, picks up his knives from the grass and runs to the gate. He throws the knives over the fence into his own yard, opens his neighbours' gate and steps out into the blinding lights of the police jeep. There are two policemen in the jeep, on the front seat.

'Are you Mr Chari? What's the problem here?'

He does not know how to begin. He makes many false starts. They are here to hear what he has called them to tell them, but the strands of his story weave into one flimsy rope of hurt and frustration. The policemen hear him out, then ask him, 'So what have you called us here for, man? Is it about this man you say died in the silver Cronos, or about your wife and children, or about your *vatezvara*, whom you say has wronged you?'

'It's all a racket,' says Farai. 'Don't you see? It's a big greedy racket and many big people will be exposed and shown for what they are.'

'Where is your wife?'

'I don't know.'

'And your children?'

'I took them to my sister's house.'

'How old are they?'

'Eight and six.'

'The law will find you wrong there. Children of that age are supposed to be looked after by their mother. You could be charged for kidnapping. Why don't you get counselling, or find a lawyer? You've wasted our time. Go and sleep on it, man, and if you have anything you can prove come to Police Headquarters tomorrow.' The jeep drives off.

Baba Jeni calls from across the fence, 'Is everything all right, Mr Chari?'

'Yes! Yes!' he answers impatiently, going back into his own house. He spends the night trying to piece together all the elements of this gigantic puzzle. He has all the pieces, but they won't join together. He wants to make the penultimate statement. He wants to have all the scandalous chefs rounded up. He wants to have the executives of the sprouting new investment companies investigated. He wants to write derisive posters about nagging in-laws and hang them up on the fence of his *vatezvara's* plot. He wants to speak out against spousal selfishness and unimaginativeness. He wants to write a treatise against hypocritical churches. He wants to give interviews on the radio. He wants to write the script for a movie that will tell it all.

5

At twelve the next day the mechanic starts reassembling his car. While he waits he goes out to look at the traffic. The blue Corolla stalks him. It emerges from the shops, ever so slowly and approaches the garage. At the gate it gathers speed and darts towards the north, only to reappear in the east. Simultaneously there are several blue Corollas, two or three perhaps, coming and going and reversing, droning like planes taking off, patrolling the area. For whole minutes they vanish, only to reappear in a convoy, before disappearing again.

He sees three young girls holding bread loaves and bunches of spinach and says, 'Have you seen the blue Corollas? It's Veronica, trying to slip out of the country, but they've got the borders manned. She's driving so many cars at once, so many decoys, she'll never get away with this. Can you help me write up the posters and we can all stick them on the trees?'

A middle-aged man in a grey shirt, well worn jeans and sandals walks into him and says, 'Farai!'

He hugs the man and clings on to him.

'Farai, do you know who I am?'

'Sekuru Tumai, of course,' he says, laughing. He knows Sekuru Tumai, his late father's uncle, a police officer at the dog section.

'Why, you remember me, then,' says Sekuru Tumai.

A scooter approaches them and he hails it. It slows down and stops, next to them. The officer riding it has a white and blue helmet.

'The blue Corolla is somewhere around here,' Farai tells the officer. 'Can you radio Headquarters and have them seal up the area?' The man nods and scoots away.

'Come, let's have a Schweppes Oranges in the shade,' says Sekuru Tumai, taking some money out of his purse. 'What are you doing here?'

'They are fixing my car at the garage. It's almost ready.'

'Are things OK at home?'

They sit on the grass and he tells Sekuru Tumai everything, about the silver Cronos and the blue Corolla, about his wife and children, and about the news on the radio. He tells him about the thumping, marching noises in the ceiling, the black, and brown dogs on the highway and his persistent dreams of being trapped in a mire of human waste. He tells him about various funerals and the crowds that are threatening him.

Sekuru Tumai takes it all in and then asks, 'Does your sister Tindo know about all this?'

'Tindo. Oh yes she does.'

They go to check on the car. It is ready. Farai pays the balance, plus the reassembling fee. Sekuru Tumai carefully inspects the invoices and receipts and monitors his change. Then, at last, they get into his car, but the passage to the gate is blocked by another car.

'Get this car out of the way,' Farai tells the mechanic, fury in his voice. Just then a young couple parks a Datsun Pulsar at the gate, blocking them in still further. Farai bangs hard on the bonnet of the Pulsar and says to the couple, 'Can you get your squeaky little wheelbarrow out of the way? I want to get out of this damned, fucking garage!'

The manager overhears him and snatches the keys out of his 323 through an open window. 'You are becoming violent again,' he charges. 'You are not going away and I'm calling the police.'

'I'm a policeman,' says Sekuru Tumai, showing his badge.

'That's what he's been doing to me every day,' says Farai. 'Intimidating me and writing inflated invoices.'

'You've no right to detain his car. Give him his keys back.'

'I don't think he is in a condition to drive.'

'That's not your problem. I'll drive him myself. I'm his uncle.'

After much hullabaloo the exit is cleared. The manager hands over the keys and Sekuru Tumai slowly inches the car out of the yard. When they are safely out, Farai winds down the window and yells at the couple, 'And if you are planning on leaving the city don't even think about it, because all the roads are manned!'

Sekuru Tumai stops at the side of the road and says, 'I'm taking you straight to Tindo.'

'But I'm all right, Sekuru,' he protests. 'I'm going there, anyway, to check on the kids. But first I have to stop by the house and make sure everything is OK.'

'You won't stop anywhere. You'll go straight to Tindo. I'll phone her to make sure you've got there. If I wasn't going on night duty I would come with you.'

Sekuru Tumai gets out the car. Farai moves over into the driver's seat and turns on the engine.

Oh how nice it is to be back on moving wheels again, with the steering wheel solidly in his hands.

***

He spots Wilbert's pick-up truck cruising on a side road, about fifty metres parallel to him. He waves and toots but Wilbert does not see or hear him and accelerates out of view.

After turning left into his drive, he runs straight towards a lorry loaded with bricks that is straddling the road. He swerves to the right and narrowly misses it.

He arrives home and parks in the yard. Baba Jeni's gardener greets him from across the fence. Entering the house, he checks the mail. There is the newspaper, of course, bloated with the latest instalments of ritual murders, corruption in high places, baby snatching, bungling new farmers, and so on. Nothing new. There is also a reminder for an unpaid electricity bill and a review of one of his books sent to him by his British publisher. He skims through it to see if it's favourable, and then casts it into a tray already overloaded with discarded mail.

In the lounge the hi-fi switches itself on and he hastily switches it off, shouting, 'Shut up!' He checks the windows and the curtains in all the rooms and then goes out through the French doors and locks up the house. On the veranda black beetles buzz round his head and he beats them off. The noise drives him mad. He gets back into the car and drives out. The sun is about to set. The rush hour is at its height. Cars crawl along the roads at a funereal pace, bumper to bumper. He avoids the city centre. On the outskirts the noise of traffic and people is less strident. Night is falling on the city.

He does not hurry. He wants Tindo to be home when he arrives. He wants to do what Sekuru Tumai said. Tindo is his mother's daughter. Tindo knows everything and will explain everything. Then he thinks, 'Why did she make all those elaborate plans for the children, and not come for him? Perhaps she is already part of the big racket already? Perhaps she too, is planning something sinister behind his back. Why did she and Shepherd dump him on the streets, like this?'

He switches on Radio Zimbabwe to catch the news, but the reception is impossible. He twists the knobs until he finds a crystal clear station. DJs, Eric Knight and Mzala, are on the air, spinning new discs. The songs are fast and rhythmical – aimed at adolescent listeners, but a subtle rhythm underlies them all. The two DJs talk fast, jesting and bantering with each other as if this was the only sensible thing left to do in the whole world. Their voices are laced with sinister overtones which make Farai squirm in his seat.

'Mzala, wati wambotamba nhova here?' says Eric.

'Aiwa, sha.'

'Manje nhasi our friend has had it. *Aigochera pautsi chaipo.** His scalp is going to dance, for sure.'

'But, Eric, why can't he see what's happening to him?'

'Too much book knowledge, that's why.'

'They've got him trapped like a rat, and he has nowhere to go.'

'Absolutely nowhere. All his friends and relatives have dumped him. They are playing a game of draughts that he can't follow. D'you know what people like him need to bring them back to their senses?'

'What, Eric?'

'A thorough whipping.'

Farai stops the car, switches on the passenger light and peers at the back seat. No one there. He switches the light off, gets out and steps back from the car. In the gathering dusk, three figures approach him, humming church hymns.

'Good evening,' they say to him.

'Good evening,' he replies. 'Are you going to church?'

'Yes. Can you take me to a priest?'

'Sure. Why do you want to see a priest?'

'I want him to pray for me.'

'Come with us.'

'Today you will see miracles,' says one of them. 'There is no one who comes to our church that doesn't get help.'

His soul flutters with hope.

At the corner of the street they turn into the churchyard. There are

---

*Mzala, have you ever had scalp problems caused by dehydration?
No, my friend.
Well, today our friend has had it. Like braaing your meat on smoky wood.

cars parked everywhere and he nervously looks away from them. The church is full and brightly lit with large, arched, tinted windows. People are singing. The boys take him into a room at the back of the church and two of them sit with him while the third goes out to fetch the priest. The boys are barely seventeen, school leavers, perhaps. Outside in the yard a tubular bulb suddenly sputters and explodes like a firework, spraying a purple shower over the cars.

The boy returns with a slender, stooping man with a face like a knife and mournful eyes, and a small, pot-bellied man with a goatee. The two men shake his hand.

'I am Brother Jacob,' says the man with a stoop. 'And this is Brother Siwela. The priest is busy right now. How can we help you?'

'Can you pray for me?'

'Before we can pray for you, we need to know what your problem is.'

'My life.'

'Your whole life?'

'My whole life! I do not know where to go or what to do, or what is happening to me.'

'Where have you come from? Where do you live?'

'Can you just pray for me?'

Brother Jacob places a finger on the tip of his nose and searches Farai's face with his mournful eyes. After a long minute, he mumbles in his colleague's ear, then he says, 'Very well. We will pray for you.'

The two men put their hands on his head, pressing his scalp and his temples with the tips of their strong, hard fingers. They pray aloud together, each uttering his litany, but every now and then their voices unite in an urgent refrain. They pray long and loud, pressing hard against his head, so their many fingers massage his skull, kneading the deep empty pain inside him. He feels better already and does not want them to stop.

But they do stop and the man with a stoop says, 'Come to our service.'

He follows the two men into the church, into another service. There are smartly dressed young people in their twenties and thirties, all clutching Bibles and rocking to the sounds of the organ. Men and women are in the same pews, all singing, chanting and moaning. In the pew right in front of him he sees Mainini Goto's nephew, Johns, in profile. This is the very Johns he grew up with in the townships, who wanted to be a journalist, but ended up in the States learning to be a lay preacher. Farai touches him on the shoulder but Johns takes one look at him and turns his face away. Everybody turns away from him.

The singing stops, people sit down and the preacher takes to the podium. He's a man in his late thirties and Farai knows him because they went to the university at the same time. His name is Pastor Wiseman Phillip Matambo and he drives a gold Mercedes. Today he is clad in an immaculate grey suit and red tie. In the bright light his forehead glistens with good health and clean living. He is preaching a sermon about the prodigal son.

'There was not a dress he let by unnoticed and unlucky was the woman he did not chat up. He frequented all the bottle stores, night clubs and shebeens in the city, burning up his money like old stationery with the matchsticks of his fancy. He craved sin and rigorously bedded with it, feasting on the scum of the land. And when he had squandered all his money on harlots, and his wife and children had deserted him, when he was ragged, hungry and poor, when his hair was matted with lice, his soul crumpled with guilt and all the heroism had evaporated from him, he decided to return to his father's house ...'

That crowd again. A tide of Alleluyas and Amens. Voices shouting in unison.

Farai.

Him, the prodigal with the rasta hair, worming his way out of the pew, to the front, kneeling on the warm floor, in front of the podium.

Him, who had made a name for himself, and spoilt it all.

Him who had shat in the Lord's face.

His head is bowed, his eyes closed, his lips open, trembling. He does not hear the cheering behind him. He does not see other people come out and join him on the floor, like a flock of multi-coloured sheep. He feels the pastor's soft hands gently, firmly, kneading his scalp.

***

After the service, the two men offer to drive him to his car. He looks out of the window of their purple Hundai Excel, driving away from the other cars leaving the churchyard.

His 323 is still there, where he left it, its tail lights flash red in the gloom.

'You left the car doors unlocked,' says Brother Jacob throwing open the driver's door. 'See, there is nobody in the car. Do you want us to drive you home?'

'No,' he says.

'Do you have somebody at home who can take care of you? A wife or relative, perhaps?'

'I'll be all right.'

'And you know your way around here?'

'I'll find out.'

He starts the car and follows them to the main road. A garage pops up ahead and he turns into it to refuel.

'Be sure to come again to our church tomorrow,' they tell him. They leave him at the garage, paying up.

He starts the car again and searches for the turn to Tindo's house. He has no idea where he is. The street signs have been stripped away by thieves, to be melted down and sold to the emergent alchemists. He peers into the dark and goes back and forth, advancing and reversing. He passes an old dilapidated swimming pool and a round-about; a huge white cement cross looms out of the vlei to his left, like a giant headstone in a cemetery. Slowly he retraces his way to the main road.

He joins the cars going to west. Ahead of them he sees Pastor Wiseman Phillip Chitambo's golden Mercedes. He looks behind him and sees a purple Hundai Excel. He is trapped in the convoy of cars going west. West where the sun sets, where the funeral will be, where they are all going to bury the man who died in the silver Cronos. They bury people with their heads facing the west and their legs pointing to the east. The west is where life ends. He does not want to go west. He wants to make a U-turn, but there is very little room to manoeuvre. Cars are whizzing past from the other direction. He chances it. He makes a sudden a U-turn, swinging the car round so sharply that it almost overturns. He swings a hard right and it rolls into a ditch, narrowly missing a white car coming from the opposite direction. Brakes squeal and shriek and cars hoot at him. The white car accelerates eastwards. The car's tail lights swell, shrink, blink and turn bluish ahead of him. He follows it.

The radio turns itself on and Stevie Wonder sings:

My love is...

The white car turns left and left again and he follows it. He must not lose it. Each time its tail lights swell, shrink, blink and turn bluish and Stevie Wonder sings again:

My love is...

They approach red traffic lights and the car slows down. He pulls into the adjacent lane and it tranforms into Wilbert's white pick-up truck. He toots and waves but an old man with white hair just glances once at him and then stares ahead. The traffic lights turn green and the truck trundles away.

He drives on, searching for a beacon. He passes chicken houses, movie theatres and the streets slowly become familiar. He approaches the broadcasting station. The broadcasting station, of course! That's where the music is coming from. He must go in at once and ask them why they are playing this music, talking about him *and* slagging him off.

'Don't park near the entrance!' shouts a soldier with a gun.

He reverses a little and stops the car. Before he can step out, Veronica's Corolla zips past and she screams from the window, 'Don't step on the ploughed-up turf!' He jumps out of the car, clear of the belt of turf and runs, leaving the keys in the ignition and the headlights on. On the other side of the road a combi waits. The moment he thrusts his face in the doorway the passengers turn their faces away from him, in unison. He backs away.

A Pajero pulls up in front of him and his friend Phillip calls out from the window, 'Farai, is it true what we heard, that you died yesterday?'

Away at the market place, an ambulance wails. He plods past the Pajero, away from the broadcasting station. At the corner there are a few people waiting for combis, but they ignore him and he slips past. He spots a photograph on the ground, in the dust, and picks it up. He holds it up, in the yellow street. It is a black and white, head and shoulders shot of a woman. She is ageless – she could be twenty-two or thirty-five. She looks like somebody he has known for an eternity, but he cannot remember her name or where he met her. Her short, groomed hair looks like Piri's, her nose like Fatima's, her large, earrings like Matiedza's, her eyes serious like Rudo's, and they are secretly pleading for something he cannot fathom. Her mouth is familiar, fleshy and promising like Veronica's. She is Everywoman.

He puts the picture in the breast pocket of his shirt. He will live with this woman forever, spend an eternity with her.

Now he is behind a cluster of township houses. A man and a

woman hold hands in a garden, their voices like water among leafless covo shoots and dried up maize stalks.

'Don't worry,' he says to them before they can look away. 'I'm just a good ghost passing by. Love each other and good night.'

He takes the picture out of the pocket again and looks at it. Something about the picture tells him the woman is dead, just as he is. She is dead and now he can live with her forever, gazing at her picture and hugging it to his breast. Now that he has found her he can lie down and find rest.

He walks on till he reaches the township cemetery. He climbs over the low fence. He pinches grains of sand to his tongue, bites a leaf and chews a tassel of elephant grass to get a taste of the underworld. No difference here. Or is he still alive? The forest of tombstones sways, inviting him in. In the distance he hears the singing and drumming of *zvigure*, the masked dancers, welcoming him.

On the road, the blue Corolla screeches to a halt and Veronica screams out of the window, 'You fool! See what I told you! You never listen and today you will know! Get out of there!'

The Corolla flies off again. He stumbles out of the cemetery, over the fence. His jeans catch on the barbed wire and when he extricates himself the zip tears at the crotch and he tastes blood on his fingers. He sprints down the road, back to the broadcasting station. His car is still parked at the side of the road, the driver's door open and the headlights ablaze.

'Don't step on the ploughed turf!' Veronica screams again, from nowhere.

He leaps over the ploughed turf, right into the car and starts it. It hums and coughs twice, then kicks into life and surges forward.

***

He is on the eastern side of the city now. His late brother Dzimai strides along the pavement beside his car, beckoning him along and he follows him. Dzimai wears the same grey suit that he,

Farai, had given him after he'd dropped out of university to walk the streets; the suit they had buried him in, but his feet are bare. Dzimai strides ahead with schizophrenic haste. Dzimai points out a pharmacy and he draws to a halt. But when he gets out the shop is closed and the doors are locked. He rattles the huge padlocks on the iron doors but nobody hears him. Dzimai hovers like a shadow on the pavement. Then he melts away and settles like a vapour on the passenger's seat beside him.

'Son of my mother, I was like this before you. Let me show you the way home.'

Dzimai, like a vapour on the passenger's seat, guides him, wordlessly, through the deserted city streets; they are homeward bound.

***

At the gate of his house, Dzimai floats out of the car like a wisp of smoke, into the night.

Thomas, the gardener, emerges from the gazebo, hands him some mail and vanishes into the shadows. He enters the house through the French door and switches off the alarm. His mother calls him from the girls' bedroom and he fetches water from the kitchen tap – refrigerated water hurts her throat – and he goes and sits with her, on the edge of the bed, while she takes cautious sips from the glass. There is no whiff of wasting flesh in the bedroom and no logos on the sheets. The bed is empty. But she is there. He hugs the pillows, pats the mattress, arranges the bottles of morphine on the side table and kisses her on the forehead.

Next door, Thomas Mapfumo thunders away:

Vane mudzimu havarove woo, heewo wo
*Vane mudzimu havarove woo, heewo wo**

---

*Those possessed by ancestral spirits never die, heewo wo
Those possessed by ancestral spirits never die, heewo wo

In the lounge the French door is slightly open and the curtains are breathing like skirts. Outside the women are coming in groups of two's and three's and pausing at the gazebo, whispering. He goes out and takes one of them by the hand and leads her into the lounge and they all follow, one by one, and he waves them in. They sit on the sofas and on the carpet, waiting for him to speak. He fetches glasses and drinks and serves them; puts music on the turntable.

'Shhh. Remember I am dead and the neighbours must not know. This will be our close secret and you can come here every night.' The women sit quietly, sipping their drinks. They are dead too, all of them, wiped out by the plague. They have come here to reminisce. They are dead and there are no more plagues here, in this cocoon of the dead. There are no bodies here. His brother Dzimai is dead too and the women are wailing at the cottage, where they laid him out in a cheap coffin. And his older brother Garai is in the study recovering from a huge epileptic fit. Their mother is wiping froth and blood from his mouth. His brother is ranting at him.

'The trouble with you, Farai, is that you've always been a materialist. All you talk about is money, money, money. You think you can win people over with your cheque book. You whinge about the people you've assisted, how you looked after mother and Dzimai and all that. Yes, you can have back that paltry sum you gave me to help me build my house. Yes, you'll have it back. Whenever I can get it. And look what this Casanova business has done to you. Who's going to wash your body now? Who's going to lay flowers on your grave? You are nobody without a wife. You have no conscience, no spine, no respect for yourself. You've never been a role model for anyone. Wait till I die and leave you to run this family. You'll be a disaster.'

Farai is sick of this tirade and he returns to the lounge. All the girls have left in embarrassment and the curtains are fluttering at the

French door. He peeps outside and sees the blue Corolla burning on the grass, smouldering into a pile of blue ash next to his 323 and he knows he must run , run from this place of death and ashes.

He locks up the house and leaves the keys at the gazebo with Thomas and drives off to The Calabash to find the girl with the shaven head, the tiny skirt and the books. There are a few cars in the yard and the bar is about to close. There are three men inside, at the counter, and they fall silent when he appears. His favourite barman looks away from him and goes on counting the cash from his till. On the shelves the bottles of spirits and wines glimmer at him. He asks for a quart but the barman shakes his head and goes on counting his money.

He leaves and gets back into the car. Under the trees outside the gate the beam of his light catches a man and a woman flagging him for a lift. He stops and opens the back-door for them and they climb in.

'I got away,' he tells them. 'I had to get away. Did you hear about it? Her car finally caught fire and melted to ash.'

In the dark the couple says nothing.

'Did you see a girl with a shaven head? I'm looking for her. They are burying me tomorrow and I don't have much time.'

The car purrs along. There is no need for questions or directions. The car knows the way. Somewhere in the night, the car stops. The man at the back holds some money to his face and he says, 'Don't worry. I won't need that now.' He turns his head and the couple have vanished already. The back seat is empty.

Now he knows where to go. There is only one place left and if Dzimai were here he would show him how to get there. Dzimai, who had spent months inside, locked up. The car knows the way. Dzimai marches at the side of the road, in the dark, leading him on. Dzimai is the black dog and the brown dog on the tarmac, wagging him on. He goes straight up the road, crossing intersections. No lights swell, shrink and blink in front of him. Stevie

Wonder does not sing.

At the hospital, he turns into the annexe. The gates are wide open. He stops the car under the trees, gets out, and leaves the engine running. The annexe walls are sheets of iron. There are no windows. He cannot find the doors. He bangs on the iron walls. Five women with shaven heads, dressed in white sheets, fall from the sky and surround him. From inside the iron walls Thomas Mapfumo's deep voice bellows, 'Hey, those who blunder into the places of the dead die!'

He bolts towards the car. He reverses out of the park, back onto the road, towards the east. The west is where they bury people, where the convoy went. The east is where the city centre is. But he must avoid the centre. He must curve back and go somewhere leafy and secluded where it will not be too embarrassing to be found. He must drive out to the farms where they are calling him to meet his fate.

He slows down. The car knows the way. It purrs past the veterinary hospital and the university. It purrs past the garage and the School of the Deaf. It glides on down, westwards.

Please, car, don't let me down now, baby. Just a few more kilometres, please.

Just before a major intersection, the car turns off the road, rolls onto the grass and stops. He checks all the windows and doors and reclines his seat. He has shut himself in and now he cannot get out. No one can get in. No, he will not get out to be ridiculed. He will stay here and foil their attempts to humiliate him and tarnish his name. He will stay here forever, cocooned from their malice. He shuts his eyes and starts the count to eternity.

One, two, three, four, five.

Five, four, three, two, one.

This is eternity, counting forward and backwards. Forever. Forever? Till when? This is his hell – he, the man who had it all and messed up. This is his hell and he will live through it, if only his mind can allow him to rest. This is his hell but he can still see the world outside.

The car radio switches itself on and Kate Bush's voice soothes a pleading Peter Gabriel who is in the depths of despair. Farai is Peter Gabriel banished from the world. The singer's voice intones in his head:

Don't give up
No reason to be ashamed
Don't give up
We're proud of who you are.

Outside, above him, two street-lights twist their iron necks to giggle and gossip. Two dwarf trees hold hands and waltz down the middle of the road. A crane demolishes houses and loads the rubble into waiting trucks.

In the rear-view mirror, his father picks at his teeth and guffaws.

He counts the numbers again, in millions, back and forth. Advancing and reversing, reversing and advancing. He wishes the crane would demolish his car and his head and finish him off, so that he can be reduced to nothingness. So that his spirit can be freed into space.

Aeons later, the crane is still smashing up houses, the whole city, and loading the rubble into waiting trucks. The trucks are scrambling away in reverse, to dispose of their load. The sun is coming up for the zillionth time; the face of his father fades away from the rear view mirror. A combi pulls up beside him and out of it disembark hurrying, dispersing feet. Thomas Mapfumo sings from the combi:

Huyai muone zvinoitwa muroyi!
*Huyai muone zvinoitwa muroyi!**

It is him, him the sorcerer they want. Him they are going to chas-

* Come and see what is done to witches!
Come and see what is done to witches!

~ 88 ~

tise, all those faceless people with hurrying feet, those people rushing to fetch whips.

He jumps out of the car and runs.

'Keep off the loose turf!'

Who said that?

He leaps over a strip of cultivated turf. There is nowhere to go. He hauls himself over the security gate of a house and hangs there; the spikes and pieces of broken glass cemented onto the wall scrape at his belly and tear his feet. He falls, picks himself up and scurries towards the road.

***

A yellow Pulsar stops in front of him and Clara, the wife of his best friend Wilbert, stands over him and calls, 'Farai, are you all right?' He crouches on all fours, panting. She leads him back to his car, but he wants to run, and run. She opens the doors and says, 'See. There is nobody in the car. Here, sit down. I'm going to find Wilbert. I won't be a minute.'

He sits on a stone breathing in huge gulps of air, waiting. The crane has disappeared and the rumbling of the trucks full of rubble is fading into the distance. Wilbert drives up in his white pick-up truck and says, laughing, 'What's up, Sir? Had one too many? Can you drive? Get into your car and follow me slowly. Buck up, man. We'll get you home.'

He cautiously gets into his car, starts it and follows Wilbert's truck. He knows the streets; the houses are familiar. The houses have risen out of the rubble. This is his suburb; there is his house, untouched by the crane. Wilbert escorts him into his suburb and says, 'Stay here. I'm going home to get my ID and I'll be back.'

On the veranda, the two winged beetles buzz in his ear. Sharai is talking to Maria inside the house. But where is Ticha? He wants to go inside but he has no keys. In the cottage, his brother Garai is simultaneously ranting and having his morning fit. They have removed him from the study and placed him here, where visitors cannot hear him. The cottage doors are locked. He searches in his pockets but can't find his keys. He shakes the screen doors but they won't budge.

In the garden a dove coos and the sound of it stabs him in the chest. The throbbing of his heart slows down. He slouches to the fence and climbs over into Baba Janes's yard. The green blur of Baba Jane's gardener watches him, motionlessly. Mai Jane closes windows and bangs doors shut. He opens the gate and collapses to his knees.

Cars drive past in the road, inches from him. Stan whizzes past in his purple 405, so close that his wheels almost crush his fingers. Chiedza vrooms away in her white hatchback. Chiri's Sunny changes gears as if about to stop, then zig-zags away. Chenjerai's Golf approaches sturdily, then indicates and turns into a close. Musa trundles past in a truck full of granite. Irene toots and waves as she goes the other way.

On the other side of the road, city council men in yellow overalls are at work, digging up the turf at the edge of the road. Their tools make grating, scraping sounds. Some of them are shoveling asphalt from the back of a yellow truck that has a flashing blue light on the top, like an ambulance.

'Ts, ts, ts, too late.'

'Nematambudziko veduwe.' *

'The cemetery closes early on a weekday, does he know?'

'What a waste.'

He rises to his feet and staggers, backwards, to his own gate. His elbows slide up the corrugated grooves and he hangs there, spread-eagled, daring the first cracks of the whips.

Then two things happen at the same time. Baba Jane pulls up in his twin cab and Wilbert jumps out of the pick-up truck in front of him.

'Wilbert,' he gasps. 'I've got exactly five minutes left.'

---

* Condolences to you all.

6

At the private doctor's rooms the patients stand aside and the nurses lead them straight through. The doctor is a light-skinned young man with a faint beard and a head shaved as clean as a rugby ball. He is the drummer in the jazz band which he and Matiedza went to see the other day. Today he is wearing a white T-shirt with the inscription BED FELLOW and tight blue shorts and green sneakers. When Farai says, 'Hello, Shasha,' he does not answer, but puts a hand over his eyes and salutes him. In the plastic paperbag under his table there is a half full bottle of gin and he opens it and takes a swig. When Farai holds out his hand to ask for a sip the doctor hits them with a broken clarinet.

The doctor listens to his chest with his stethoscope, tests his blood pressure, makes him open his mouth to say ahh and push out his tongue. He pulls down his jeans to have a look at his penis, pumps it twice, nods, then scribbles something on the palm of his hand.

The doctor goes out to the reception to talk to the nurses, comes back and gives him two toffees and a female condom and bows him out of the room.

The nurses whisper in Wilbert's ear and then Wilbert hurries him back to the car.

All along the road, pick-up trucks follow them. They are loaded with his furniture, and his household goods. This one has sofas, that one the dining room suite, this one has the beds, that one the fridge and stove, this one the TV and hi-fi, that one the computer and books. And there are empty pick-up trucks speeding in the other direction, like motorised dung beetles, to collect more of his stuff. Damn it, Thomas has given them the keys and they have broken into his house and are cleaning him out.

'Wilbert, stop!'

Wilbert fills in some forms at the hospital reception and keeps an eye on him. The trucks keep coming and going, coming and going and he stands helpless at the entrance, watching them. The hospital orderlies pull him away and lay him on a table to take X-rays. Outside police sirens wail as their jeeps try to control the traffic. He sits up on the table.

'Now, Farai,' says Wilbert.

'Wilbert, you fool! Can't you see what they're doing?'

'Just lie on the table.'

The machine X-rays his legs, his feet and his chest.

In the corridor a child screams. Ticha! That's where they've kept him all along! They are operating on his son Ticha, taking out his liver! Just like that girl in the papers whose kidneys they stole. He bursts into a room just to catch the nurses whisking the child away, and the nurse aides in pink cleaning up the blood. He follows them to the next room and a naked, bony old woman with shrivelled breasts stares blankly at him.

'Get up and run, Gogo!' he yells at the woman.

Something trips him and he falls, too late, and faces in white shirts surround him, leering down at him. He hollers and struggles but they pin him down with firm, powerful arms. Something pricks his arm and he shudders and collapses.

***

He opens his eyes slowly. He is lying in a bed, and his three sisters Tindo, Bertha and Kata are sitting on a bench beside him. He winks and waves at them and chuckles, '*Muri bho?* I hope you guys bought me a really nice coffin, none of the stuff that rots after a few years.'

Kata, the eldest, starts crying and Bertha says to her, 'Now Sisi Kata!'

'When did you come?' he asks.

'Yesterday,' says Bertha, cleaning her manicured nails. 'We couldn't find you at home, so we went to sleep at Tindo's place.'

'How did you two find out about me? I died last night.'

'Tindo called us.'

'How are my children, Tindo?'

'Fine.'

'How long have I been in this bed?'

'Not very long. You hardly closed your eyes.'

'Where's Wilbert?'

'He's filling in some forms at the reception.'

A young nurse comes by and he says to her, 'When can I go, nurse? It's my birthday today.'

The nurse looks at the three women and asks, 'Did you bake him a cake?'

Tindo says, 'A very big one, but he can't have it, unless he gets better and comes out of here soon.'

'Happy birthday,' says the nurse.

He sits up and tries his legs. They feel fine. There's nothing wrong with him. Two bouncers in white shirts and trousers approach the bed and one of them says, 'Do you want to come and talk to the doctor, now?'

'He came to pretty quick,' says the other. 'Do you think we should give him another jab?'

'No, he's fine.'

The doctor sits at the end of the corridor, interviewing patients.

She is an ample woman in her early thirties, with high faced cheek-bones, rings on four fingers and long braids that she keeps tossing back from her face. The queue is long. She is slow and thorough with her patients. Wilbert comes in with two black bags, smiles at the bouncers and joins them. When the doctor eventually calls Farai in, they all want to go with him but she says, 'No, I want him by himself.'

'*Hes* Pesvu,' he says to the doctor. He went to university with her and knows her well. She was a wisp of a woman then and people used to make fun of her name. One day he had played tennis with her. On another occasion when he had tonsillitis he had gone to the surgery, where she worked as an intern, for a prescription and promised to phone her.

She smiles weakly at him and looks at his forms and says, 'So what brings you here, Mr Chari?

'You ask him,' he says, pointing vaguely towards Wilbert who is sitting outside in the waiting room. 'He dragged me here while they were out there ransacking my house.'

'Who was ransacking your house?'

'My enemies. They're all jealous of me.'

'What do you do?'

'I'm a writer.'

'But I mean, what do you do for a living?'

'That's what I do. Writing.'

'Do you make enough to live on, this way?'

'Does it matter?'

'Now let's go right back to the beginning. Tell me how your problem started.'

He goes into reverse gear and tells her everything. He tells her about the accident and the postponed shooting of his film, about the news on the radio and the car crashes, about the church service and the convoys, about eternity on the night road and the pending whip-lashing. There is a terrible logic to his narrative, but she does not see it. She nods her head and lets him roll, while she writes notes on a card. Then she goes to the waiting room and calls Wilbert over and whispers to him. Wilbert comes in with the two black bags and goes out with two small green ones! Farai feels a tweak deep in his crotch and he says to him, 'Look, Wilbert. You fool! Can't you see what they've done? They've stolen our dicks!'

***

Dr Pesvu discharges them and they go out in a bunch to Wilbert's pick-up truck. At the exit the film crew is waiting – finally. The cameras are trained on him and the overhead lights blaze down. The cameramen are invisible, behind the lights. He stands stunned in the yellow heat but Wilbert grabs his elbow and marches him on.

'Too late now,' he turns back to yell at the cameras. 'You left it too late and now I have to go. You'll have to look in my archives!'

Out in the park a little boy cries as he is bundled away, round the building, by a group of nurse aides.

He sits with Wilbert in the driver's compartment and his sisters climb into the back of the pick-up. Wilbert reverses out of the park into the road. His sisters' dresses billow in the breeze. At the gates a security man with a shirt like a policeman's stops them. Wilbert shows him some papers and the security man lets them through.

They turn right and drive through the open gates into the hospital annexe.

'Not here, Wilbert,' he says. 'We're lost.'

Wilbert stops the car and comes round to open his door for him. He is not moving. They're in the wrong place. What are his sisters doing? He can see them moving slowly towards the steps of the building. It is a prison. It is a trap. He shouts loudly. 'Stop.

Stop, we're in danger.' They do not turn round. Wilbert's hand is pressing on his shoulder. He twists away and bangs his head on the door frame of the car. This is a conspiracy. He is being kidnapped. He shouts for help but no one hears him. Wilbert is becoming an enemy. Part of the racket. Wilbert has his hand on his shoulder, Wilbert is urging him out of the car. Wilbert is pressing him to walk. He can hear voices, his legs move but his spirit is shouting and his mouth is silent. The walls of the annexe are not made of iron and there are windows and doors, people moving inside, voices talking. There are no women with shaven heads, wrapped in white sheets, tumbling from the sky. Tindo knocks on the door.

Wilbert holds him tightly by his elbow.

I could slap you in the face, Farai. Hard. At first I thought you had one too many and now this – you shaming us both with the nonsense about people ransacking your house and the orderlies stealing our dicks and you refusing to co-operate. So, is this what madness is about? Stripping off our thin disguises and exposing our deepest insecurities. Fancy you – that immaculate little government schoolboy with whom I used to study. Remember, we went picking mazhanje *together and later, courted Letwina and Clara. Who could ever imagine you would end up like this? Yet you were always quiet, sometimes, keeping to yourself and studying yourself half blind, writing precocious, melancholic poems about God and the universe as if the impending weight of the ending world was upon your shoulders. You the belated virgin imagining yourself Stephen Dedalus's twin in James Joyce's* A Portrait of an Artist as a Young Man! *(Remember we did the book in the sixth form?) Maybe you should have pursued something more practical, like accounts or business administration rather than stick with literature. Look where it has landed you. Yet I fear your instability is real, very real. Something I can't fathom.*

Hey, do you remember our classmate Peter Twetwete and how he ran amock when somebody inadvertently revealed to him that the woman he had all his life assumed to be his mother was really his stepmother! Remember how Peter had to be withdrawn from school? I wonder what became of him! I wonder what triggered your downard spiral. I've warned you frequently about being reckless with your life. We never talked seriously about the problems in our families as friends. I should, I realise now, have encouraged you to open up. I fear Veronica might have been too hard on you, getting carried away with her church stuff and refusing to give you room to be yourself. But perhaps you drove her back too hard. No woman I know, Farai, wants to stand back with folded arms watching her house fall apart.

Pull yourself together, man. Do you think I don't have problems as well? Are you the only married man in this world? What would you do if Clara and I weren't here to help you?

Get a life, man!

***

In the ward, a nurse fills in his details and hands him half a tumbler of coloured pills to take. She gives him blue pyjamas and a blue gown and Wilbert helps him change in a closet. The pyjamas are too small and have no buttons – Bertha finds him a safety pin to secure the front but his pants show through the gap. She takes his clothes, his purse and his keys. The kitchen staff bring in lunch – or is it an early supper – and offer him a plate. He tastes a finger of the sadza and beans and pushes the plate aside. Kata says to him, 'You must try and eat.'

'You must go now,' he tells Wilbert. 'You have had a long day.' And he says to his sisters, 'You too. You may go now.'

He walks them to the doors. The bouncer at the door unlocks the door and lets them out. He waves to them and smiles, and the bouncer shows him back into the ward.

'You must be Mike Tyson's cousin,' he says and the bouncer nods and smiles.

In the large sitting-room, people in blue pyjamas and blue gowns are sitting on chairs. The room is dimly lit, the small light bulbs are deep in the ceiling, winking bluish. He finds a chair near the wall. The padding of the chair is soft and warm in his hands, and when he sits on it his crotch vibrates. He tries another chair and it is warm again and his crotch vibrates. In the basement of the building under his feet cars are revving up, and going in and out. At the front in a well-lit cage two men in white are stand watching over the room, and a young female nurse sits writing on cardboard cards.

Round the corner, past the cage, up the stairs, there is a band playing. He walks up to the cage and says to one of the men in white, 'Doctor, are we allowed into the show?' The doctor shakes his head and points him back to the ward. He is young, slim, and wears gold bracelets on his wrists. He has a small tattoo on the nape of his neck.

He goes back to look for a chair that does not vibrate. All the free chairs are warm and they vibrate. He sits on the floor and his buttocks vibrate. All his insides vibrate. The doctor comes over from the cage at the front of the room and pulls him up by the wrists, back onto a chair. It is warm and he begins to feel the warmth inside his belly. He feels under the chair for the knobs to adjust the heat.

The people in the room are very quiet. John White, the albino soloist, shuffles about with his guitar strapped to his shoulder, looking for a cool seat. The slim doctor comes out and presses him down onto a chair. John White starts strumming on his guitar but his music is drowned by the noise of the band. The slim doctor comes over and takes his guitar and locks it up in the cage.

He goes over to the cage again and says, 'Doctor, when can we go and listen to the band?'

The doctor says, 'When they've finished tuning their instruments.'

He goes back to his seat and waits. He waits and waits and waits. The people in the room are very quiet. Down in the basement the cars are revving up more loudly now, impatient to get their passengers into the show.

In the cage the nurse looks at her watch and says something to the doctor. The slim doctor comes and takes his hand and says to him, 'We can go now.'

He takes him to the cage but not up the stairs where the band is seated. Nobody is going up the stairs because the show is full. At the bottom of the stairs Mike Tyson's cousin stands waiting, to keep out gatecrashers.

'Doctor, are we going to the show now?'

The doctor leads him down a long corridor with lots of rooms – booking rooms in this seedy hotel. He opens the door of one of the rooms to have a look. The room is empty but for a picture of a woman taped to the wall. He does not know her. She is very beautiful, but she scowls at him with piercing cat's eyes.

He screams.

The slim doctor takes him out and leads him into another room. There is no light in it. He peers into the dark. The doctor pushes him in and locks him up. He hears the clinking of keys in the lock and then the flap flap of his shoes as the young man walks away. He screams again.

The room is pitch dark. He can't see his hands or his legs. He gropes around the walls for a switch. They are solid iron and there are no doors, windows, or grooves to greet his fingers. He bangs on the walls. There is no sound, no echo. He shouts out. His voice does not bounce back at him, but tinkles like broken glass at his feet. He cannot tell how high or how deep the room is. He feels the floor with his hands and feet. Wood. Warm wood. There is faint tremor under his hands and knees, that vibration again. He huddles into a corner.

He hears a tiny noise seeping up, almost impossibly, through the floor. A distant sound wave – music. The band is playing, their music is very faint, but growing steadily louder. Louder and louder, growing in his ears, until he can hear the clarity of the mbira's melody, and the clashing and banging of the other instruments.

Thomas Mapfumo is on the stage and the crowd is cheering. He is chanting questions. Piri and other singers answer with a refrain.

And who's the biggest wordsmith in this land?
Farai.
And who's the biggest storyteller in this land?
Farai.
And who's the biggest lover in this land?
Farai.
And whose is the biggest heart in this land?
Farai.

The crowd cheers and the refrain is repeated twice.

In the basement a lone car, a Corolla, revs up, angrily, impatiently, revving to leave, to get out this place.

Mapfumo straightens up and brushes back his dreadlocks. The girls sweep up to the front of the stage for the next verse. Fatima, in a white cheesecloth dress, purple doek and black high-heeled shoes, mounts the stage from the dance floor and grabs Piri's microphone. Mapfumo stares at the upstart. Mike Tyson's cousin advances from the shadows backstage but Mapfumo waves him off. The dancing girls step back. Fatima stands at the centre of the stage, swinging the microphone cord clear of her feet, waiting to answer Mapfumo's questions. The singer raises his microphone to his mouth, cues her and begins the verse again. He chants the questions and Fatima answers.

But who's the biggest snob in this land?
Farai.
And who's the biggest coward in this land?
Farai.
And who's the biggest clown in this land?

Farai.
And who's the biggest dick in this land?
Farai.

The crowd roars with laughter. Fatima hands back the microphone and steps down, onto the dance floor.

In the basement, the lone car breaks through the gates and speeds away in shame.

A snake wriggles out of a hole in the wooden floor, slides slowly into his pyjamas and wraps itself firmly around his waist like a belt. He does not scream or shout. He is numb with the words of the music, and reeling with embarrassment. He only feels the snake when it is there. The snake tickles his navel with its fang, licks the tips of his breasts and brushes his lips. The snake is not hot or cold, it is only a slippery presence. It undoes itself and slides back into its hole. The snake is a messenger shuttling back and forth, between this iron-walled prison and the stage, between him and Fatima. The snake is the go-between, carrying back strings of forbidden red, white and black beads from Fatima's waist.

Out on the stage, the rhythm of the *zvigure* takes over.

7

A terrific knock jolts him and light floods into the room, burning through his eyelids.

'Get up!'

His neck is stiff and his limbs heavy as logs. His eyelids are glued together. His head is somebody else's. He claws at the open door to support himself to his knees. In the corridor men in white go from door to door, rattling keys, pounding on doors and yanking door handles. Rubbing his eyes, he struggles to his feet. Men stumble out of the rooms, some naked, others half dressed and stagger to the end of the corridor. Dazed, he steps out and follows them.

In the bathroom naked men stand around a large tub, waiting their turn. They go in two's, like cattle at a dip-tank. The water trickles from a single tap and they share a piece of brown carbolic soap and a tiny green towel. One or two of them have their own soap and towels, but they do not share them with the others. Nearly all the men sit in the tub with their bums in the water to soap and wet themselves. Some of them scoop up the water from the tub and rinse their mouths.

When Farai's turn comes he goes in with a short, dark man whose face is covered with pimples. Mr Pimples offers him his tablet of Vinolia soap. Farai accepts the soap and rubs himself with his hands, but he does not sit in the bath. He pulls out the rubber stopper to let the scum go and scoops the warm water straight from the tap with his hands. He waits until Mr Pimples climbs out of the bath, then scrapes away the cakes of dried blood on his navel and between his toes. When he finishes Mr Pimples holds out a large, thirsty blue towel to him but Farai shakes his head and wipes himself dry with the legs of his pyjamas.

In the dormitory one of the men in white shows him his bed and locker. Each man makes his own bed. They are arranged in two rows, against the walls. His is neat and already spread, covered by a thin, white cotton gauze. It has not been slept in. There is nothing in his locker except a Gideon's bible. Mr Pimples comes over with a tiny bottle of scented Vaseline and squeezes Colgate toothpaste onto the tip of his little finger.

They all then clean the dormitory. They do the windows and the walls first, with newspapers and wet cloths, then the lockers and the floor. In the ward Peter Ndlovu struts out with a black and white football in his arm and plants the goal posts with two dustbins. He arranges the players into two teams. The two linesmen in white wait with their flags on the opposite side of the fields. In the cage the football officials argue with each other until the match is cancelled. The spectators go away grumbling. The men decide to play hockey. John White, the albino, struts up and down the line, holding his broomstick to his mouth and singing.

In the dining hall, the matron calls them up one by one to give them their pills before they can have breakfast. The young trainee nurse carefully counts his dose into a tumbler and gives him a glass of water to take them with. The trainee nurse is nervous; the matron is waiting to find fault with her, waiting for her to drop a tiny little pill on the floor. Wanting her to do everything correctly at once. The matron is grumpy, as if she has had a fight with her husband or a relative has died or is very sick.

When he gets to the counter he holds out his hand and says to the matron, *'Nematambudziko,* Matron.' She glances at him and turns away.

They sit on the tables to eat breakfast. He is sitting between Mr Pimples and a woman with short hair, large eyes and a huge scar down the length of her arm. There are several women among the tables, all wearing blue night-dresses and gowns. Mbuya Masibanda is serving steaming porridge on tin plates and milk in little yellow jugs.

He shakes Mbuya Masibanda'a hand and says, 'Mbuya Masibanda! When did you transfer from Mpilo? I didn't know you were working here! How is Sekuru, and how is Mainini Nomsa?'

'Zvauriwe!' Mr Pimples warns him in low, urgent tones. *'Zvauriwe,* you never listen. Don't touch that milk.'

Farai puts down the jug and digs into his porridge. He asks the woman next to him, 'What happened to your hand?'

'Fits,' she says. 'I fell into a fire while I was having an epileptic fit. Paraffin stove. Nearly burnt my arm off. I've had them since I was a toddler. They say if you get burnt by a fire while having a fit you'll never be cured of them. Do you believe that?'

'I don't know.'

'My mother took me to a man, one of the best herbalists in the land and he wouldn't touch me because of the scar. Got a cigarette?'

'No. Are you allowed to smoke here?'

'They can't stop us. My, my, my. You must be really hungry, lapping up your porridge like that. They must be giving you multivitamins. Do you want my plate?'

'What about you?'

'I don't like porridge and I don't usually eat in the morning, unless I've had a puff. You are new here, aren't you? I know everybody here. Been in and out and in and out for nearly a year, now. Did you bring any hot stuff?'

'No.'

'Next time your folks come over tell them to bring you a half of Bols, or Black Label. It's easy. You just slip it into your pyjamas and hide it inside your mattress. A few tots of that will do you wonders at night. My friend brings me one every now and then. Better than the poison pills they are feeding us. Are you feeling stiff and groggy?'

'Yes.

'Don't worry. You'll get used to it after a few weeks.'

Mbuya MaSibanda takes away the plates and hands out large tin mugs of tea and thick chunks of buttered brown bread.

Mr Pimples whispers to him again in urgent tones. 'Don't drink that tea! It's got milk in it!'

Miss Fits overhears him and says to Farai, 'Don't listen to him.'

Farai wolfs down the bread and the rich, sweet, steaming tea. Mbuya MaSibanda hands him another mug of tea and two more chunks of bread and says to him, laughing, 'Eat, Muzukuru. I don't want a puny man who can't fend for me when your uncle is dead.'

***

In the garden he stretches out on an iron chair in the warm sun, undoes the belt of his gown and closes his eyes to collect his thoughts. Everyone is sitting in the garden. Mr Pimples walks towards him: a grey waistcoat over his pyjamas, a pipe dangling between his molars, and the day's newspaper in his hand. He plants his chair opposite his, against the wall.

'Here you are,' he says, holding out the paper in the breeze. 'The dollar has been devalued again, and two primary elections postponed. Farai takes the paper and tries to skim through an article: SIX GOLD PANNERS DIE IN DISUSED MINE SHAFT but the paragraphs seem to have been pasted upside-down.

'I've been looking for you to tell you what a nutcase you are. How could you guzzle all that milk at breakfast time, like a little calf that's been locked away from its mother for a week. Spoiling it all at the last minute, when everything has been arranged. How come you never listen to your folks?'

Mr Pimples takes out a packet of tobacco and fills his pipe. Farai squints at him and notices that he has a gold ring on his left hand.

'You want to listen to my story?' Mr Pimples says. 'You want to know how I messed up? You think I have always been like this? Would you believe that I was once the secretary of a large company? The managing director did not like me and thought I was out to get his post, so he went round the country to find things to fix me with. First time I collapsed on the table in my office; then my right eye went blind and my right wrist numb; then I started hearing voices each time I showed up in the boardroom. I started walking, talking and shouting in my sleep; then I couldn't sleep at night. I couldn't go to work for months. The MD campaigned to have me fired, but the board agreed to put me on half pay. My wife ran away to live in a flat, leaving me with the children. My folks tried everything, doctors, herbalists, *n'angas*, and *biras*. Nothing worked. Then one day a little old woman came from nowhere to my house and said, "I know your problem. I can help you." The woman took me to a river and washed me. Then she had me sweat in a blanket, kneeling over pots of boiling tubers and gave me bitter medicines. She said, "Young man, the person who did this to you put bad herbs in your milk so you must not drink milk until your treatment is over." I took the medicine she gave me, stopped drinking milk or anything with milk in it, and very soon started feeling better. I went back to work and worked as usual until one morning the MD called me to his office, and offered me a cup of tea. There were other senior people in the meeting. The manager was all smiles, and told me that I had got a salary increase. His secretary brought in cups of tea. The tea was rich with milk. I forgot about it. I was too excited. Or rather, I was too embarrassed to say no. I took one sip and started feeling dizzy. I passed out and had to be taken home. That night I could not sleep and started talking to myself, shouting, hearing voices. They brought me here again. My family looked everywhere for the little old woman but they couldn't find her. Then we heard she had died. Nobody could help me. And here I am. One little mistake did it. That's all.'

Mr Pimples scratches his face, knocks the tobacco out of his pipe and reloads the bowl. 'Listen. I'm an older cousin of yours. You don't know me. Aren't you of the porcupine clan?'

'Why, yes,' says Farai. 'How did you know?'

'Shhh. Not so loud. Walls have ears. Your problem is my problem. It's the problem of the people of our clan. Our brains are allergic to milk. I want to help you to avoid the mistake that I made, so the whole clan does not die off. I want to teach you to listen to your folks. I want you to listen to me, so that you can go back out there and carry on with your work, writing books.'

'How do you know I write books?'

'See, you're just a little boy. You know nothing. I knew who you were the minute I set my eyes on you.'

Mr Pimples frantically searches the pockets of his waistcoat and his gown, turning them inside out. 'Damn it, they took my matches and now I have to beg for every single stick. They think I want to burn down this place.'

Mr Pimples goes off muttering to the cage and does not come back.

A young girl, no older than fifteen, alights on a stoop and chants at the cage, 'Do you know me? Do you know me? Do you know me?'

Peter Ndlovu goes round the garden shaking people up to form a football team but it is too hot to play now.

John White picks at his flaking red lips and strums on his arm.

Sekuru Sithole fixes a hose to the garden tap and starts watering the flowers. Farai says to him, 'Sekuru Sithole, is it going to rain this year? Have you bought your seed and fertiliser yet? There's going to be a huge grain shortage, you know.' Sekuru Sithole comes over in his squelching gumboots and pats him on the shoulder, then taking out his *chipako*, shakes snuff onto his palm. Farai pinches the snuff with his fingers and loads it into each nostril. He sneezes.

'Way to go, Muzukuru,' Sekuru Sithole says.

Miss Fits flops onto the empty seat next to him, with a pen on her ear, an old magazine and a half completed crossword puzzle. 'What do you call a person who brings a case against another in court?'

'Plaintiff,' says Farai.

'And what do you call a person whose sexual or religious beliefs are eh, opposed to what is considered right, or eh, normal? It begins with a 'p'.'

'Pervert.'

'You are very good at this.'

'Not really. I'm too lazy to be good. Do you do this all the time?'

'It keeps me busy. Whenever I travel to Jo'burg or Lusaka to order or sell my stuff I can do puzzles for hours on the bus.'

'Is that what you do, buy and sell?'

'Yes, sir. I don't wait for no man's money. But the customs people make things tough for us, seizing our stuff, demanding bribes and treating us like common thieves. It makes you want to become a border jumper. I jumped the border once, going to Mozambique with a group of women. The night was dark as charcoal. The border patrol fired at us and we ran. One girl died on the spot. She was my friend. We gave ourselves up and they locked us up like common criminals in cells that stank like pigsties. That night I had two attacks. There wasn't a hospital nearby, so they let me go.'

The slim doctor comes over from the cage and stands over Miss Fits, waiting.

'Time for my phenobarb,' she says, standing up.

Farai wanders into the sitting room to look at the magazines. They are old and have no covers. Mountain climbing. Car racing. Fashion. Cookery. Music. Stella Chiweshe pops off a soiled page, with her mouthful of flashing teeth, glittering robe and beads; plucks at her mbira. Oliver Mtukudzi pauses and coughs his TB cough. Michael Jackson whines and Eddie Murphy grins like a good African.

There are a few people in the sitting room, on chairs. There is a TV at the end of the room and a dark woman with large black buns of plaited hair sits watching the blank screen and writing something in an exercise book.

'You there,' the woman calls out to him. 'Which side of which triangle is the hypotenuse?'

She holds up the exercise book to his face. The double spread is full of drawings of all mathematical shapes – equilateral and isosceles triangles, squares, rectangles, pentagons, rhombuses, prisms, with definitions neatly written underneath. On the other pages are mathematical theories and equations.

'You don't know what is meant by hypotenuse?' she says again, chuckling sympathetically. 'Sit down and I will teach you.'

He sinks onto the chair beside her, hypnotised by her voice. He feels her small hand on his chest, inching down to his navel and searching inside his underpants. Suddenly the TV turns itself on and a newsflash voice with a Chinese accent yells, 'Yes, Yes, Hualing III is finally approaching the planet Zobus. Yes, we've made it. Yes, yes, yes.'

On the screen Hualing III, a glowing red shaft, approaches the large iridescent ball of the planet Zobus, first slowly, then faster, faster and faster till it plops into an amorphous sea of colours.

His head is euphoric with the landing. He is part of it; he is the astronaut of that spaceship getting sucked into that vortex, the architect of the adventure of the millennium.

'Mwazvita!'

Mike Tyson's cousin stands over them and pulls Hypotenuse away from him.

'Get off, Mwazvita. Go and wash your hands at once. You there. What are you doing? Are you all right?'

Farai sits up in his chair and stares at the blank TV screen. His pyjamas are open. His belly is wet and slippery. He rubs it with his gown.

***

In the room behind the cage the drums of *zvigure* beat faster and he sees the feet and the shoes of the men shovelling grey earth into the gaping hole on the floor. He staggers to the cage and asks the slim doctor, 'Who has died?'

The slim doctor says nothing.

'Is my *vatezvara* dead?'he asks again.

The slim doctor says nothing.

He goes out to the garden for some fresh air. Cloud covers the sky and the earth is bathed in semi-darkness. A dove coos at him from a bough somewhere, and the sound of it pierces his heart like a needle. His breath is shallow, raspy like a chameleon gripped in the tight vice of human hands. His knees are water. The slim doctor pulls him up and stands him against the wall. He leans against it, rocking with the movements of the ship.

This is a big swaying ship with buildings, dormitories, gardens, trees and people on it and the slim doctor is the captain. The people in the cage are the crew. The ship is as big as a football field, so big that they he cannot see the sea. He can hear the waves lap-

~ 111 ~

ping up on the sides of the ship. They are going to Jamaica to eat coconuts, breadfruit, pork and goat meat, and lie on white beaches; already he can hear the wild, welcoming sounds of reggae, calypso and samba. Yes, they have left behind Zimbabwe and its woes.

The captain gives him some pills and a tumbler of water and says, 'Here, take this and sit down for a while. You must be sea-sick.'

At lunchtime the matron hands out more pills. She smiles when he gives her a little salute. He sits at the table between John White and a small, light-skinned man who is very quiet.

'You are Mazitulela, aren't you?' he says to the small man. 'Your father was our headman at Gwehava Village and he gave my mother a huge field.'

The small man looks at him and says nothing.

Mr Pimples sits at the far edge of the table, scratching his face. Farai looks for Miss Fits but does not see her. Hypotenuse sits at another table, poring over her exercise book and when her eyes meet his she smiles and looks away.

Mbuya Masibanda piles sadza, covo and bones on his plate and tells him, 'There's more for you when you finish this. You'll need it because your folks are coming to see you after lunch.'

8

After lunch the visitors start arriving. He has the biggest crowd in the annexe – Tindo and Shepherd, his sisters Bertha and Kata, his brother Garai and his wife Maiguru Mai Emily, Wilbert and his wife Clara, Veronica'a sisters Maidei and Maiguru Mai Winnie and Babamukuru Baba Winnie, Veronica's mother and father (his *vatezvara* and *ambuya*), Mainini Goto and his cousin, Faith, Sekuru Tumai and his wife, Veronica herself and a female friend from her church. They all enter in a row and shake hands and stand or sit around him in the garden.

The matron leans out of the doorway and he says to her, 'Sorry Madam Matron, *nhasi matsikwa nembhombhera!*'*

'No, no, it's all right,' says Madam Steward, 'But we normally allow only two visitors per patient at a time. How are you all?'

Mbuya Masibanda and Sekuru Sithole bring extra chairs and he introduces them. 'Mbuya MaSibanda and Sekuru Sithole look after us,' he says, and for the benefit of his brother and sisters he adds, 'Mbuya MaSibanda has just transferred in from Mpilo and Sekuru Sithole used to live in Gwehava Village, remember?'

A suitable silence follows, then his *vatezvara*, the oldest and most auspicious person in the gathering, coughs and asks him, 'So, how are you feeling now?'

'No, I'm fine. I'm fine,' he says. His *vatezvara* is a good man, a

*Today you have a trainload of visitors.

well-meaning man of God and the memories of the gaping hole and the tirade against fathers-in-law made by the DJ on the radio makes Farai twinge with a strange shame and guilt.

The visitors do the inevitable round of inquiries. He is amazed at the turnout and somehow fortified by their presence, but is embarrassed to be the cause of all this fuss. He knows these are his folks, the people who would matter if something happened to him. He turns his heavy head slowly to survey them. Tindo's velvet shoes next to him seem very dark and very large. Maiguru Mai Emily is quieter and more deferential than usual. Garai leans against the wall, waiting to fire the first missiles. Ambuya sits to attention, like a hen guarding its brood from fleeting shadows. Baba Winnie laconically pares his nails. Wilbert is ready to volunteer his seat, or to offer a drive to anyone who needs it. Veronica, in an open-necked beige corduroy dress and blue sneakers, sits inscrutably at the far end of the right, swinging plastic bags between her legs and expecting the first accusation.

'Where are Sharai and Ticha?' Farai asks.

'We left them in the car,' Maidei replies.

'Children are probably not allowed in the wards, but we can ask,' Mainini Goto advises.

Tindo, Maidei and Faith get up to ask the matron if this is possible, retrieve car keys from Veronica, and return with Sharai, Ticha and Nyasha. Farai hugs the children and plants them on his legs.

'What's wrong with you, Sekuru?' Nyasha asks. 'Are you sick?'

'Headache.'

'Are they giving you Disprin?'

'Yes, and more.'

'So you are eating and sleeping here?' Ticha asks.

'Yes.'

The children stay for a few more minutes, before being escorted out.

Mainini Goto says, 'Just take your medicine and eat your food, *nhaika*, and you'll be all right. But I think you need a haircut. Did you bring his pyjamas, Mai Rumbi? These hospital ones are too small for him.'

His *vatezvara* says a prayer, then he and his wife leave, saga-ciously. Garai announces that his Ph.D. celebration party is in two weeks time and invites everyone. His wife, Maiguru Mai Emily, remonstrates, 'But, Baba Emily, we can't start worrying about that here, now?'

Garai wipes his nose with his fist and says, 'I'm sure he'll be out by then.'

Veronica's sisters leave. Wilbert and Clara also stand up to go. Mainini Goto has an appointment with a customer at her knitting shop. Veronica's friend has another patient to see at the main hospital and hands over a large, Get-Well card.

Sekuru Tumai and Kata plant their chairs in a semi-circle around him. Veronica is called over. It is time for family matters. Sekuru Tumai rolls up the sleeves of his shirt to the elbows, preparing to skin the beast of the problem. 'Mzukuru, we are glad to see you're getting better. What you've gone through is extraordinary. I wasn't happy when I saw you at the garage two days ago. I talked to your brother and sisters. You are responding well to hospital medicine but we need to do more. I, as your uncle, think that as soon as you get out, we should go around a bit, to the old people who know; those who can see into the mists of time, and seek help from them.'

'The next two weekends are out for me, with the date of the grad-uation party already set,' Garai announces. 'And I have a field trip lined up, after that.'

'Your sisters are here,' Sekuru Tumai tells Garai. 'They can come with me on your behalf.'

'If a patient says "I'll get better," then he'll get better,' says Bertha.

Farai tilts his head vacantly.

'It doesn't mean we give up on hospital medicine, of course,' says Sekuru Tumai, relenting a little. 'Well … you can think about it.'

'This morning Kata and I had to go to your *vatezvara* and *ambuya* and beg them to let your wife return home.' Garai tells him.

'Thank you for that,' Farai says, cautiously.

'It's not your thank you's we want, but a commitment to change. And we hope this shows you that it's not always money that talks. You ought to listen to your wife and siblings.'

'Don't talk like that, Muzukuru,' Sekuru Tumai cautions Garai.

Farai is too tired to protest, or explain. He turns to Veronica and says, edgily, 'So you've come back? Where were you, sweetheart?'

'Mukoma Farai!' Bertha protests … The whole thing threatens to burst into a typical Chari family confrontation.

'Did you get the phone disconnected? And did you change the padlocks on the French door? Did you see my car keys? Or my Visa card?'

'See?' says Garai, half triumphantly. 'He's here sick but he's talking Visa cards already! Money, money, money!'

'Some people forget they haven't paid back what they borrowed,' Farai pants.

'You can have your money back this month-end, Babamunini,' says Maiguru Mai Emily, raising her head for the first time.

'After five years!'

'Shakespeare said, 'Neither a borrower nor a lender be,' Bertha chips in, half-vengefully.

The argument is threatening to degenerate in an all too familiar manner. Farai holds his head in his hands. Sekuru Tumai leans back in his chair, surprised, searching his palms for a way out of this new dilemma. The matron appears again in the doorway and leans out towards them, wagging a finger at her lips.

'We are straining the patient,' Kata says, peaceably. 'We didn't come here to argue. The patient is getting better and *sekuru* says we could try other options later. Let's just leave it at this for today, shall we?'

Veronica hands Farai a paper bag with toiletries in it and another with apples, oranges and bananas. He wants to hold her hands, or even hug her, but something stops him.

'Did the woman with the green Golf phone you?' he asks her and she shrugs.

Suddenly something snaps and he grabs the paper bags from Veronica and flings them hard against the wall. Squashed fruit tumbles out; toothpaste, Vaseline and lotion scatter all over the grass. Bertha says, 'Mkoma Farai!' Veronica stomps off in anger. Tindo picks up the strewn items and hands them back to him. Garai helps himself to an apple and a banana, saying confidently, 'See you at the party.'

At the door Mike Tyson's cousin lets them out and points him back to the sitting room. From the window he watches them climb into the cars and drive away in a small convoy, Sekuru's smoking green Datsun 120Y in front, followed by Maiguru Mai Emily's Peugeot 405 and Veronica's blue Corolla with its rattling exhaust. On seeing Veronica's car he shudders slightly. In the garden a dove coos feebly and he slaps a bee from his ear.

***

'How can you bring your whole clan like that to see you?' Miss Fits laughs at him, in the garden. 'It's as if you were at a wedding, or a funeral. Was that your wife you shouted at when you threw things at the wall? Huh!'

'How did you know?'

'She's very beautiful. Does she love you?'

'So, so.'

'Why were you shouting at her?'

'I don't know.'

'It's the pills they're giving you. The pills cleaning up the rusty wires in your brain. I know how you are feeling. I hope she understands. You'd better get well soon and get out of here before she runs off with the *sascams* out there.'

'Did you have any visitors?'

'Just one. The woman I go with to Mozambique. My folks are tired of visiting me. They think I'm play-acting, acting nuts, and having fits on purpose. My friend brought me something, though. Look.'

Miss Fits stands up and peers around to make sure no one is watching; then lifts her dress up to show a bottle of brandy held between her thick black pubic curls and white pants. 'You want a tot?'

'I'm drying out.'

'Or do you want my body? We could always lock ourselves up – or run off for an afternoon.'

'I want to get out of here fast.'

'OK. It might mess up your pills. The moon is going to be full this week and I might have an attack. I always have an attack when the moon is full. Might as well snap off when I'm drunk. Shit, imagine. Thieves broke into the room I rent and stole my bed and my boom box. I think I know who they are too. Kids who live in my street. School-leavers, just imagine. They know I'm locked up here.'

'What will you do?'

'Don't know. At least I can stay in this *sascam* place while I think of what to do. Hey, can you play table-tennis?'

'A little.'

'Come, I'll show you.'

She takes him to a room behind the cage, where they had the burial in the morning. Two men are playing at the table, and he inspects the tiled floor for traces of funereal soil. Miss Fits books a game but when their turn comes he moves heavily and cannot return her balls fast enough. He places the bat on the table and sits down. He watches while she plays with another male patient.

After supper, when it is beginning to get dark, he goes to the sitting room to watch TV. He tests the seats. They are cold and they don't rock. He looks for somebody to talk to. Mr. Pimples is grumpily holding his head and staring straight out of the windows. Mazitulela is reading a tiny Bible in the corner, alone under the lamp. Miss Fits is nowhere to be found. Peter Ndlovu is playing draughts with Taxi Driver – a thin man with a scar on his forehead. Do-You-Know-Me? is quietly knitting something in her lap. Hypotenuse is leaning back in her seat, staring with her eyes at the ceiling, an open exercise book held to her breast.

On the TV, villagers in front of burning shacks are being bundled into waiting lorries by policemen in riot gear.

He goes to the cage and says to the slim doctor, 'Where did this happen?' The slim doctor says, 'I don't know.'

He says again to the slim doctor, 'You're not a doctor, are you?' And the doctor says, 'How do you know?' He says, 'Because you are too slim. You must be an orderly.'

He says to the woman in the cage, filling in a pile of khaki cards, 'You look like Matiedza.' She says, 'Who is Matiedza?' And he replies, 'A film-maker friend of mine.'

She adds, 'I'm not Matiedza. I'm Sister Nondo.'

'You admitted me here yesterday, or the day before, didn't you?'

'Good, now you remember.'

'Everybody is sleeping. Can I talk to you, Sister Nondo?'

'Right now I'm busy. We can talk tomorrow. Go and watch TV.'

He goes back to his seat again and watches television. On the screen it's time for The Nation. A tall man with a strong neck and large powerful hands is saying something and banging his fist on the table. The man is a minister in the government. He knows the man because he went to University with him, and one day when they met in the States the man had left his two pretty little daughters with him so that he could attend a workshop. The daughters had called him Uncle Fari and rode on his knees and pulled at his locks while he bought them Coke after Coke. Now he is trying to remember the man's name. He wonders if maybe he can phone him and ask him to come and take him out of this place. He cannot hear what the man is saying because he is talking too fast and is angry about something.

He yawns and starts dozing. Everybody in the room starts dozing. Mike Tyson's cousin and the slim doctor come and lead them to the dorm. The women go the other way, with Sister Nondo.

The slim doctor shows him to his bed, and rolls back the sheets. He is very tired. He hauls himself in and closes his eyes.

***

When he wakes up in the morning Mazitulela is lying on his back in the bed next to him, reading his tiny Bible. Mazitulela does not answer when he greets him.

They go to the bathroom to wash as before and when he offers his towel to Mazitulela, the latter looks aside and continues rubbing his body with his hands. At the cage the slim doctor fetches him his Vaseline and toothpaste, which they are keeping for him, and a dozen hands reach out to share his toiletries. Mr Pimples shouts them off.

'*Mabhoyi!* Leave him alone. You think everything here is free company rations. Free, free, free. Free education, free health care, free food, free sex. Free AIDS. We passed that stage long ago.'

He snatches the Vaseline from Taxi Driver and the toothpaste from Hypotenuse and hands them back to the slim doctor for safekeeping. Then, to Farai: 'Wake up, man. You think these people are your friends but they are just parasites.'

At breakfast he again has two mugs of tea with milk and several chunks of bread. Mr Pimples glares at him with displeasure as he sips his tea. After eating he helps Mbuya Masibanda clear the table and wash up the dishes. Mbuya Masibanda thanks him and squeezes more dish concentrate on his sponge. After cleaning up he is relaxing in the garden when he is called to the cage. He has a visitor. Sister Nondo has gone and the new, day nurse says to him, 'There is somebody to see you, Mr Chari. Be quick about it because we don't usually allow visitors outside normal visiting hours.'

A young man with a black leather jacket and black bag says to him, 'I'm a barber. I have been sent to give you a haircut.'

'Who sent you?' he asks.

'Mrs Goto from the knitting shop. She says she is your aunt.'

Farai fingers his locks and says, 'I don't need a haircut.'

The nurse looks at him and says, 'You'd look better with a haircut, Mr Chari.'

'I don't need a haircut,' he repeats.

'What shall I say to your aunt?'

'Tell her what I told you.'

The barber leaves. Farai feels good, saying no and sending him away like that.

Soon afterwards, Thomas, his gardener, calls in. He is wearing his Sunday best.

'I've come to see you,' says Thomas. 'I heard you were not well.'

'Thomas! Where have you been all along?'

'I was home at night, guarding the house and then sleeping during the day.'

'Did you talk to me?'

'Yes.'

'What did I say?'

'Each time you came home, I said, "Manheru Daddy". You would greet me, and ask, "How are Sharai and Ticha?" Then I would give you the mail. But you mostly talked to yourself. Later I picked up two knives in the garden and gave them to *mhamha*.'

'Did you see a bank card? A Visa card?'

'No, Daddy.'

'You came all this way to see me? Have you got money for the combis?

'I borrowed some from the boy next door.'

'Oh, Thomas. How nice of you to come.'

He borrows money from the day sister and gives it to Thomas. Soon afterThomas has gone, who should arrive but a third visitor, Wilbert's wife, Clara.

'How are you today?' she says. 'You look much, much better. Veronica and I went shopping and she asked me to bring you these.' She hands him a pair of brand new pyjamas in a paper bag. 'Try them on so that if they don't fit we can go and change them.'

He goes to the dormitory and changes into the pyjamas and comes back to the cage, trying to swing like a model.

'Perfect,' says the day nurse. 'The hospital ones were so small and tight on you that your *ambuya* didn't know where to look!'

Farai does not have any pyjamas at home. Perhaps the last pair he had was when he was at school in Form 1. He likes to sleep naked, 'like a maize cob stripped of its leaves,' his mother had frequently warned. 'What will you do should you fall sick at night or at a wedding, a funeral or at your *ambuya's*?' Now he feels good; he likes the purple design and the feel of this new pair. It's good to have things bought for you by other people, especially when you're in hospital.

'Clara, did Wilbert pick up one of my bank cards? A Visa card?'

'He didn't say. I'll ask him when I see him. I've got to go. I'm running for a meeting.'

After Clara has gone, he asks the day nurse if he can use the phone.

'We don't allow patients to use the phone unless it's urgent,' says the day nurse. 'Who do you want to phone?'

'A friend. It's very urgent. Please.'

'What's the number?'

She dials the number, listens for a second and hands him the receiver, through a hole in the wire.

'Sisi Maud,' he says. There is nowhere to go and the day nurse and the day slim doctor can hear him and are listening and have to listen to what he has to say. 'Maud. Hi Maud. It's Farai. How are you? I'm fine. Yes, I'm fine. I'm back for the summer break. I can't tell you where I am right now. No. No, I'm not at the Beitbridge border post. No, I don't know what noise you can hear in the background. No, I'm OK. Of course, I'll see you soon. Listen, Maud. I'm using a borrowed phone and have to be quick. Can you do me a favour, Baby? You have the fax number of my university department in the States? Yes, the one you used to fax me on. Look. I think I've lost my Visa card and I can't contact the bank myself right now. Can you fax my Head of Department, Pauline Weeks, and ask her to call my bank and have them freeze my account right away. Pauline Weeks, Weeks as in days and months and weeks. Oh, yes, I'm fine. No, don't worry. Just do what I'm asking and I'll phone you later, and we'll talk.'

***

In the afternoon, after the games of basketball, frisbee, table tennis and hockey in the garden, the day nurse organises elections for the Patients' Welfare Association Committee at the annexe.

'There are four posts to be filled,' the day nurse explains. 'We used to have a committee but the people all got discharged. We'll need a chairman, a secretary, treasurer and committee member. It will be an open ballot and you can vote once for each post. Let's start with the position of chairman. Who would you like to be your chairman?'

Mazitulela points a finger at Farai and almost everyone puts up their hands in agreement and raises their hand. There are no further nominations and Farai is duly elected chairman and goes to the front. Miss Fits is elected secretary, after a close contest between her and Hypotenuse. The post of treasurer goes to Taxi Driver after Mr Pimples steps down, and Peter Ndlovu secures the position of committee member.

Farai sits at the front, flanked by his lieutenants.

'The chairman must give an acceptance speech,' says Mr Pimples.

'Yes, a speech.'

Farai clears his throat and digs into his language bag for a suitable register. 'It certainly feels nice to be elected chairman,' he says. 'Thank you for electing me, even though I came here only a few days ago. My plan for the committee is to work to establish better links between the hospital staff and the patients, so that we can make life more comfortable for everyone. Let me start by thanking the hospital staff for looking after us. We know what a tough job that is. They work on a tight budget, and the government is cutting back on services. Then I want to encourage the patients to take over some of the work done by the staff. There is no reason why we can't help with cooking, and washing up dishes. Some people can even help with the clerical work in the office.'

'Hear, hear!' Hypotenuse interrupts.

'Then there is the question of hygiene, in the bathrooms, for instance. In the men's bathrooms we should scoop the water directly from the tap and not all bathe in the same dirty water. Each person should have his or her own soap and towel, and our visitors should take care of that.'

'Some of us have no visitors,' says a fat man with a club foot.

Do-You-Know-Me? raises herself on the tips of her toes and chants twice, before Mr Pimples shouts her down, 'Of course we know who you are, twit. Sit down.'

'No, no, no, Baba, ' says the day nurse. 'We should not speak like that to others, *nhaika*.'

'All right, nurse,' says Mr Pimples. 'We can't have anyone talking and interrupting the proceedings. And shouldn't the secretary be taking down minutes of this meeting? Where are the minutes of the last meeting? Are we running this as a proper meeting, or what?'

Miss Fits borrows a pen and some paper from the night nurse and starts talking down notes.

'I think we ought to have a suggestion box at the office for people to put down their ideas,' says Farai.

'Hear, hear,' says Hypotenuse again.

'Does anyone have any suggestions to make?'

'I think we should have books and magazines we can read and understand, in the sitting room,' says Taxi Driver. 'I don't know anything about gardening or fashion or horse-riding.'

'As a rider of mules,' giggles Miss Fits. 'The hard MaShona type.'

Taxi Driver glares at Miss Fits, then beats a bee out of the back of his shirt.

'Not all of us have the eyes to read with, Mwanangu,' says Gogo Maghirazi, squinting in the sun and wiping her biscuit-sized lenses on her pyjamas.

'Can we play games with teams from other annexes?' Peter Ndlovu suggests.

At the end of the meeting, Farai proposes weekly meetings for the patients and promises to send all the suggestions to the Matron, through the day nurse.

'Good meeting,' the day nurse says to him.

Mr Pimples overhears her and says, chuckling and savaging his face with his nails, 'For a chairman of fools, he didn't do too badly.'

*****

At ten the next morning, Veronica arrives, without notice, to take him to the main hospital for a brain scan. She is brief with the nurses and offers to drive him there. He suggests that they walk, on the pretext that he needs the exercise. He is uneasy about riding in her Corolla, or going anywhere near it. He hasn't been in it more than two or three times since she bought it, or rather, since her company had sold it off to her as a benefit. The truth is that the car represents all he resents about his wife, and the company she works for. And in the last few days, the car has been the elusive harbinger of his fears.

So they walk to the main hospital, she slightly in front of him with the papers, and he shuffling after her. She pauses frequently for him to catch up with her and looks repeatedly at her watch. At the hospital reception she goes ahead to find out about their appointment and where they have to go to. He hates to be led along like this, in his pyjamas and rubber slippers, and looked after by somebody else. He wonders what people who know him would think and say if they saw him. He cannot remember when he was last in a hospital.

They sit waiting, not talking, outside the scan room. She does not ask him how it is at the annexe, or how the whole thing started. He remembers how one day, years back, he'd arrived late to fetch her at the hospital after she'd gone for a gynecological operation, and how she'd had to phone her father to come and fetch her. He remembers his shame and guilt, when he arrived late, to find her gone. Maybe she is now getting her own back, he thinks.

Half an hour later the door opens and a young woman with a white dustcoat calls them in.

'Are you claustrophobic?' she asks him. 'This won't hurt but it might be a little uncomfortable.'

She makes him lie on a tray and close his eyes and pushes his head into a droning tunnel for about fifteen minutes. At one point he panics and almost shouts out, but holds on till the nurse stops the machine and lets him out.

'Good show,' smiles the nurse.

'So is my brain all right?' he asks her as she hands them the negative prints.

'I can't read the prints,' the woman replies. 'Your doctor will tell you what the results are.'

*****

Back at the annexe, two psychiatrists study his cards and his negatives. One of the psychiatrists is in his early thirties, sporting a black leather jacket and a wild wing of oiled black hair. His harried looks and his accent make him decidedly Cuban. The other one is a black Zimbabwean man in his late fifties, wearing mix and match clothes and appearing to be in charge. Both doctors smoke incessantly and share cigarettes. The matron sits in attendance.

The black doctor sketches parabolas and lines on the back of an envelope and says, 'You are suffering from what is known as a bi-polar disorder. Your brain swings up and down. It's something to do with the chemicals in your head. When the activity in your brain gets high you become hyperactive. That's why you couldn't sleep and you rushed about, thinking things were happening to you, and everything happened fast. When the activity-level decreases you become depressed, moody and slow. The medicine we are giving you is to keep your brain activity in check, making sure it doesn't go too high or too low.'

'Do you drink?' the Cuban doctor cuts in.

'Yes,' Farai says, hesitatingly.

'He's an alcoholic,' Veronica lays it bare.

'Then you'd better stop. If I were you I'd give it up completely. You brain is already highly charged and drinking is like pouring water onto live wires. See?'

'I know it's difficult for him to stop, Mainini,' says the black doctor. 'But maybe you could start by giving him one or two drinks, say after supper, while he's watching TV. Make a point of buying him his drinks yourself, when you go to do your groceries. Let him drink at home. That way you keep his drinking in check and slowly wean him off it.'

'She's never bought me a beer in her life.' Farai protests bitterly.

'You are the doctors,' Veronica warns them. 'But once you allow him a single drop he'll go off and drown himself.'

'Are you two happily married?' the matron asks, bluntly. 'Because if you're not, it would be like throwing the pills into a river – plop – the medicine won't work. And the traditional option won't work either. Your folks can brew as much beer as they want and you can visit the best herbalists in the country but without you two understanding each other, the patient will never fully recover from this illness.'

'When can I go home?'

'As soon as we think you are well enough to do so. We know you are anxious to get back to work, but right now your health is more important. We'll keep reviewing your progress. Remember, take your medicine consistently.'

'And, Mainini,' says the black doctor, 'You must realise that even if he gets well, you husband is never going to be the same person again. Be prepared for that.'

'He's not the person I married, and hasn't been for a long long time,' Veronica retorts.

9

After supper, just before lights out, he goes to the office and asks the night nurse, Sister Nondo, for the phone.

'Congratulations,' Sister Nondo says to him. 'I heard you were elected chairman.'

He calls Maud and she tells him that she sent the fax and has already received a reply from the university. Everything is fine. His account has been frozen. Maud is a very close professional and personal friend. She is a writer and an arts administrator. She happens to have gone to the same school with him, and was raised in the same church. They are both Geminis and so have plenty in common.

'But where are you, Bhudhi?' she asks, anxiously.

Suddenly he has a change of heart and says, 'Can you keep a secret, Sisi Maud?'

'If you want me to, Bhudhi.'

'Well if you want to know, I'm at the hospital annexe.'

'Annexe?'

'Yes. I had a bit of a breakdown and had to be admitted. Don't worry. I'll be out soon.'

'Can I come and see you tomorrow?'

'Yes, if you like. Just remember the place is a bit unusual. Not everybody here is exactly well.'

He gives the phone back to Sister Nondo and thanks her. She is sitting with an electric heater in front of her, reading a book.

'What are you reading?' he asks.

She holds the book up for him and he can't believe his eyes. It's one of his novels, the fourth, which had won him a major prize and taken him to many countries in the world.

'You mean, here I am sleeping in your ward, under your care and you're reading my book!'

'I did it in my literature class at O-level, so when you were admitted, I already knew who you were. So I said to myself, 'Maybe he thinks too much and that's why he's like this,' and I went home and dug the book out of my trunk, so as to read it again and see what goes on in that *sascam* head of yours.'

'What page are you on now?'

'He's beating up the traitor woman who looks like his mother.'

'Doesn't that bit scare you off?'

'It sure does. How do you think all this up? It's so real, just as if you were there. It must be hard work.'

'Sometimes the ideas come, just like that, but sometimes I have to help them along. I don't know why I write. I suppose it's like beating oneself on the head with a stick, while trying to enjoy the pain, but it feels good when a book is complete and you can say, "Here it is."'

I got a 'B' in literature, but 'A's in science and maths.'

'I didn't like maths much. One time I had to beg my maths teacher for an extra mark so that I could beat Brian Sigogo to first position.'

'Why didn't you go on to do A-levels? You could have become a doctor or a pharmacist.'

'My parents were poor peasants and they couldn't afford to let me go further. It's a long story. You'd better go to bed now, or the matron might find you here.'

'Good night.'

***

He lies awake in bed, waiting to fall asleep. Perhaps it's just after eight. In the dorm several people are snoring already; a bed squeaks insistently in a corner.

He thinks.

He thinks about himself here, in this dormitory, stripped bare like a maize cob. The events of the last few days are an inscrutable blur that he must try to arrest and reconstruct. He thinks of himself here, away from home, with nothing to worry about but food, pills and sleep. No stress here, just the mindless cycle of eating and sleeping. No newspapers, no bills, no wife, no women, no children, no car, no hangovers, no police, no page-proofs, not even any dreams. He crashes out and the next thing he remembers is waking up. It is amazing how one can survive without the necessity of food and sleep – but did he survive? Would he be here if he had? How did it start?

He remembers the long months in the States, one of a handful of black professors, trying to teach creative writing and African Literature to white kids some of whom even struggled to construct sentences and paragraphs. Rich white kids, who flew past him in their twin cabs after their evening classes, slowing down as he trudged home in shin deep snow, to yell , 'Want a ride, professor?' Most of them took his classes merely to fulfil college requirements.

He'd arrived in the USA fired with enthusiasm, only to find the college machinery somewhat slovenly and indifferent. His teaching load was light, to give him time to do his own writing, and the pay was great, but he felt guilty taking the money when he thought that he was not being challenged to achieve his best. Perhaps he was just too jaded to set himself challenges. His colleagues in the department accepted him and let him be but they never really opened up to him, or so he thought. Or was it him who never opened up in the first place? Two or three of them invited him to their houses for coffee or a drink, and that was it. He had initially feared that they would expect him to be an avid spokesperson of his country and continent and the redeeming voice of that huge diaspora of the world's most misunderstood and disrespected people, so he decided to play their game and thrive in the grey fringe of their seeming indifference. After all he was a novelty: black, foreign, African, artistic and, he thought with a tinge of irony, 'distinguished'. Or 'exhausted'? 'Extinguished,' perhaps?

'You need to come out of your cocoon,' a black female professor friend from the south had often warned him. 'Loosen up and go with the flow. Go square dancing if you must. Twist and shout. Rock and roll with the mob. Even Bruce Springsteen bristles with huge ironies:

I was born in the USA

I was born in the USA.

You've got to tease out matters of race and ethnicity and not sulk or drown in self-pity. Remember the world cannot change itself for you, and you cannot change it.'

At his flat he cooked himself elaborate breakfasts of omelettes, bacon, sausages and orange juice and dinners of sadza, rice, pasta or potatoes complemented with spinach, turkey, fish and chicken. Soon he gained weight and he had to buy clothes in larger sizes. He developed a sturdy rhythm, two hours of TV after every supper, once a week to the laundromat and the supermarket, to a bar every Friday night and the movie theatre on Sunday afternoons. Some days he played tennis with colleagues from the department. He lived cheaply and sent the bulk of his salary home so that Veronica could pay the bills, and to invest in projects, which he identified. He bought presents for his wife, his children and family, and had them shipped to Harare.

He called his wife every week. One night when he was lonely and randy he asked Veronica to take the phone to the bedroom and undress, so that she could be naked with him, while they whispered to each other for more than an hour, across the time zones. When the telephone bill came, they decided that this was not a feat to be repeated.

He had time, silence and solitude, but he could not write. He was too lonely to put pen to paper, and his impotence made him feel guilty and restless. He went to the library for books, discovered exciting new authors in translation and read voraciously but remained empty and unsatisfied. He ached for company to fill the void, for the firm grasp of a bottle of Black Label in his hand, for cigarette smoke, noise, music, comrades shouting in lively argument, and the banter and laughter of people. The college was too secluded, too far north among cornfields and cattle; a place where rich, reluctant parents trusted the vital maturation of their children to the rigours of the university curriculum. There was no common room or bar in the college where the teaching staff could meet and talk, and the few bars in town were jam-packed with hordes of twenty-something students with whom it would be imprudent to fraternise.

He travelled a lot, though, jetting across states to read from his work at other colleges. He attended literature association conferences and made friends, with intelligent, large-hearted people, men and women, with whom he corresponded by e-mail. But the vast distances made real contact difficult.

On one such outing he met a young, Zimbabwean couple, Noah and Lizzie, research fellows in a large college only two hours away. He began to visit them on a regular basis, once every three weeks perhaps. They would take him out drinking, or to attend one of the numerous cultural functions that took place. After a while, he began to loosen up. At one such function he drank until three in the morning and kept Noah and Lizzie waiting while he engaged a group of guests in an ugly argument about human rights and good governance. On getting to his hosts' house he stayed up for the rest of night, recording music onto blank cassettes well into the morning. Later, after Noah had gone off to the office, Lizzie said, 'Now, Mkoma Farai, what would you like to do? Would you like to eat, or just have more to drink?' Eventually she drove him to the bus terminus and left him there, feeling like a bad guest and regretting everything in his usual, rueful way. When his bus came, the driver sniffed at him and said, 'No drunks on my bus, Sir,' so he had to board another one, three hours later, wasting precious green dollars, taking a roundabout route and arriving home after midnight. Damn the bottle!

The snow was piled high in the driveway and against the doors. On his little boom box Simply Red was singing:

And I love the thought of coming home to you
Even if I know we can't make it
Yes, I love the thought of coming home to you
Just a little ray of light shining through.

He began to count the weeks until the summer break. He crossed the days off the calendar, like a soldier on a tour of duty. His lectures deteriorated. He stopped giving quizzes and long assignments. He gave in to his students' demands and awarded high grades. 'If you give low grades here, you will work yourself out of a job,' somebody had warned him. He was ashamed that he was cheating, and began to think little of himself. He visited the library less often. He watched junk TV, listened to junk music and ate junk food. He lost his zest for cooking. He wore his shirts twice, and his jeans three or four times, before washing them, in order to double the time between his visits to the laundromat. He stopped going to the movie theatres. He packed away his tennis racket.

But still he phoned Veronica. He wanted to tell her about his loneliness and despair, but he did not know how to begin or if she would believe him.

Always, when he travelled to another country, something happened to him and this developed into a pattern that he found increasingly hard to dismiss.

On his way to Australia to receive a prize, he missed his flight, and had to re-route himself through Bangkok. In Britain he ran off with a doting, troubled Indian poetess to help soothe her soul with jazz, while the rest of the group went off to pay homage to William Shakespeare's grave. In Canada, naked in some feigned gesture of naturalism, alone in broad daylight in a canoe, he nearly overturned among shoals of seals and walruses. In Switzerland he banged his head on pillars as he swayed to Stella Chiweshe's hypnotic mbira and drugged Swiss rock and roll. In France he argued all night with a fellow woman writer about Dickensian English and patriotism. In Sweden he woke up clamped to his bed by some force, so that he kicked and banged at the wooden walls of his dilapidated little hotel room – and screamed when he saw an old, old white woman with long white hair at his door, offering him a candle. In a fourteenth century castle in Italy, his spirit floated out of his body and gazed at his prostrate self. In Germany he returned home with a sprained elbow and running nose after a group of Nazis cornered him in the street, beat him up with batons and sprayed something in his face. In Swaziland he watched a colleague's face burst into bloody pulp as apartheid police beat him up in a joint called 'WHY NOT?' He ran off, ran and ran and ran, with a Muswati woman who gave him refuge in her room and left him two quarts of beer, bread and meat while she went away to supervise Sunday-school children.

Johannesburg was something else.

In Johannesburg, in the dying days of apartheid, after a long, dreary workshop, he wondered unwittingly into a gay bar and found himself surrounded by patrons of all colours, some of whom were wearing female underwear, all parading their flesh and soliciting for partners. A young man with a blonde wig said in a rasping voice, 'Buy me a drink!' and he looked away. Her couldn't tell the time; perhaps it was early or mid-morning. A black man in a grey suit leant over him from behind, as if to order a drink, and snatched some notes from his shirt pocket. When he looked up, the man sneered at him and flicked open a knife. Sensing trouble, he rose from his seat and fled outside. Two figures followed him into an alley and one of them tripped him up. He fell onto the urine-stained asphalt. He picked himself up and ran across a street, bleating like a ram in a slaughterhouse. He jumped into an open jewellery shop and hid behind the counter. He heard the shop assistants phoning the police. He ran out of the shop, down the street. A combi was picking up passengers and he leapt into it. Catching his breath, he paid the fare. The other passengers glared at him. On the speakers Sankomota blared:

Stop the war, eh, eh, stop the war, eh eh

He rode in the combi for some time, and when he thought he was far away enough he alighted. On the streets, there were vendors selling clothes, trinkets and hot food on mobile stoves. He bought himself a plate of pap and boerwors and when he had eaten he started retracing his way back, but he was not sure which way he had come. He hesitated to ask for directions because he feared that if he opened his mouth his accent would betray him. He felt that someone was after him. The crowds unnerved him. He singled out people to approach. He tried English, then Ndebele, and an old woman gave directions in deep, impenetrable Zulu. He walked on and on, noticing that he was leaving the shops and offices behind him. He entered a suburb with high-rise blocks and clothes hanging out of windows and off balconies. He asked again for directions, and a man said to him, 'Try for taxi. There!' He went through a gate into a red brick building; at the entrance he met a young woman and said, 'Taxi, please,' and she shook her head. He asked, 'Phone?' and she answered in Xhosa and indicated with a finger that he should follow her. She led him up the stairs to a room on the third floor, unlocked the door and showed him in. He entered. There was a single bed without a bedspread, a small table and a chair. On the table there was a family size bottle of orange concentrate, a glass and a loaf of bread. No phone. The moment he sat on the chair the woman went away, leaving the door open. When she did not come back he stood up to check in the corridor. No one there. A gust of wind blew in from the open window and caused the door to bang shut. He tried the door. It would not open. It had locked itself. He banged on the door. He called out. The woman did not come. He sat on the chair, waiting. There were no built-in cupboards in the room, just the bed and the table and the chair; nothing to indicate that the room was lived in. He heard voices in the corridor and he banged on the door and called out; the voices vanished down the stairs. He waited again, perhaps for an hour and a half. Damn it, he would miss the afternoon session of the workshop.

Then he heard footsteps, the door being tried from outside, the woman shouting angrily, in accusing clicks.

'Let me out of here,' he banged on the door.

He heard the voice of another woman in the corridor, speaking in Xhosa.

'Let me out of here!' he said again.

'We no Englis,' said the second woman. 'Is you fault. Door no open now.'

The women tried a key in the hole, then a screwdriver and a knife.

'Get the spare key,' he said.

'We no spare key. Spare is for caretaker.'

'When is the caretaker coming?'

'Tumorrow mon.'

'I'm stuck here. I have to get out. Can't you go and find him?'

'We no Englis. Why you no speek Xhosa? You too proud, like

white man. Where from are you?'

'Just let me out.'

'Money first.'

He went to the window and looked outside. A roof jutted out on the floor below. A voice said to him, 'Slide down the gutters, floor by floor.'

He saw some men on the ground below but their figures were blurred. The men said to him, 'Jump, man! We'll catch you.'

'Money first,' said the second woman.

Then, suddenly, he was seized by an unbelievable idea. The top half of the door was made of opaque glass. If he smashed the glass he might climb up and wriggle down into the corridor and escape!

He could not stop himself. He picked up the chair and, without thinking twice, flung it at the door. The glass showered out into the corridor, leaving a big hole in the door.

'Now they gon teach you,' said the woman. 'You don't lissen. Now you gon see.'

Footsteps in the corridor. He climbed lamely on the chair, searching for a grip on the hole. A key was inserted in the hole, turned and the door burst open. A burly man in green overalls dragged him down, off the chair. He braced himself for the blows. The thick handle of a garden pick struck his shoulders, his back. He hugged the man. The man threw him off and hit his knees. He squeezed between the man's legs and scrambled out. He ran down the corridor towards the stairs. The man came after him. He caught up with him. He hit his head and his ankles.

He stopped on the stairs, pleading for mercy. Blood trickled from his scalp and through the foggy, crimson mist of his broken, blood-stained glasses, he saw the man's fat, bald-headed face, above him and two or three women. The man banged his ankles and toes with the handle.

'Please don't kill me,' he pleaded with the women. 'I'll pay for the door. I'll give you anything you want.'

The women said nothing. He fished into his back pocket and laid a bundle of notes at the man's feet.

The man picked up the money, counted it and said, 'What in other packit?'

'It's just my passport,' he gasped.

'Show.'

He held up the passport with blood stained hands and the man snatched it.

'You from Zimbabwe?'

'Yes.'

'Zimbabwe people stupid, come buy, buy everything here and thiefing and broken doors every way. Now everything costing more more for us here becos of Zimbabwe people.' He threw the passport at his feet. 'Now go! If I sees you here or any ways in Hillbrow, me gon kill you, for sure.'

He picked up his passport and limped down the stairs. He had lost his sandals, his spectacles were broken, everything was blurred and foggy.

Outside on the street a biker stopped to survey his injuries.

'Go to hospital, man,' he said. 'Police no gon help.'

A taxi came by and he hailed it and limped in.

At the hospital the orderlies shaved his head and bandaged his feet and said, 'What happened bro?' and he said, 'I was mugged,' and they said, casually, 'At least they didn't kill you.'

A morose white doctor stitched up his scalp without taking any X-rays and gave him anti-biotics for his wounds.

An Afrikaans woman from the workshop came to collect him. She loaded him and his wheelchair into a van and sombrely drove him to his hotel. For three days, while he waited for the first flight home, he lived in the wheelchair, fed from an open window like a chicken, by the woman from the workshop. He insisted on attending his session to deliver his paper from his wheelchair, barefoot and wrapped up in his bandages which made his head dress look like a turban. There was wild applause when he made revolutionary remarks about the use of English language by African writers, but the hesitant applause at the end of his presentation made him wonder about the value of workshops, and if writers should ever engage in debates.

When the workshop woman put him on the plane she was glad to be free of him, this visitor who had embarrassed himself and his hosts. At the airport he was one of the first people to board the plane, with children, the old and invalids. It was a short flight and he joked with the stewardesses all the way. When the plane landed he was the first to disembark – the stewards eased his wheelchair down the steps and collected his luggage.

And there, on the other side of the glass doors, was Veronica, standing astride, swinging the car keys between her knees, waiting.

***

'Why were you mugged in Joburg?' his brother Dzimai had asked, over and over again, in his cryptic tones, before he died. 'Do you think this was just something ordinary? You say you could have died. So who do you think saved you?'

***

Once, years before, his father and Dzimai had died within the same week, he went on a binge. The whole family was supposed to go to the plot for an informal Christmas gathering to commemorate the departed members of the family, to show that they were still a united family. They would do what their parents had done while they were alive and so help their name to live on. This was an occasion for immediate family, no relatives from the extended family were invited. Garai and Shepherd had gone on ahead to organise an ox to be slaughtered, the food and the drinks.

Veronica drove the children on the morning of the 23rd to meet up with Maiguru Mai Emily. He promised to follow on the morning of the 24th as he had some urgent work to finish.

He had already contributed his share of the costs.

On the 23rd he worked all day and in the evening he decided to go for a drink to relax. Inevitably, meeting up with friends, one drink led to the next. Those were the days when Fatima looked after him, when he needed her company to nurse his frayed spirits. The chain of deaths in his family following so close on each other had unnerved him. Perhaps something was amiss and he would be the next to fall. But most men don't cry, or do they cry forever?

He drove to Fatima's compound to find her.

Her door was open and she was sleeping. He sat on her bed, and shook her gently until she woke up.

'Have you eaten?' she said, and he opened a new quart. She took out a fresh fish wrapped up in a wet cloth and lit her paraffin stove to prepare it, while he listened to her small radio. It must have been after two o'clock in the morning. He told her about the trip to the plot and she said, 'You have to go. Family matters. Your mother won't be happy if you don't go.'

He ate the fish and drank some more. He could not sleep. He wanted to talk. It was as if a hole had been drilled in his head and his stories were pouring out.

'My mother died in my house, well, almost. Dzimai spent his last months in my house and died at the plot, just after we had buried my father. How could Dzimai die within the same week as my father?' he said. 'Why should all these tragedies come straight for me, as if I were the only living Chari left?'

'Because the people down under and up there know you have the means to solve the problems and have chosen you.'

'My wife thinks its coincidence. She doesn't know what I'm

going through. She keeps quoting my father, who died saying, 'No Chari should ever drink.''

In the morning Fatima fetched some water from the compound tap and bathed him. While she was out, washing his clothes, he opened her wardrobe to take a look inside. Her clothes were neatly folded on the shelves and there were a boy's school uniforms and books. He knew she had a child in Grade 1 who lived with her mother and that she worked part time as a waitress at the nearby bottle store, but he had never asked her what she did otherwise, or where the boy's father was. There are things a man just doesn't ask. He was content to play with her waist beads and eat her fish, and let her bathe him and wash and iron his clothes and hold his face in her hands at night while he talked. But she was not a cheap, ignorant girl. She was clean and dressed well. She belonged to another culture, a brave, old culture that preserved its cults and was not ashamed to train women to be real women. She was twenty-five, but already wise enough to know that the best way to lose a man was to try and own him. He liked her because she was a survivor and she knew a lot of things about places, people and survival.

But what was this tucked away at the back of the top shelf? A bottle of water with tubers floating in it! He took it down and while he was examining it, she came in.

'*Iwe, iwe,* don't touch things you don't know anything about.'

She took the bottle away from him.

'What's that, Fatima? Is this your *mupfuwhira*? Your love potion.'

She gulped down a mouthful from the bottle. 'It's a natural root that cleanses your body and opens up your mind and your eyes. It's good for all kinds of ailments. I got it from my grandmother. I just keep refilling the bottle with water. Want to try it?'

He took a swallow from the bottle, and shuddered from its bitterness. He pursed his lips, tears trickled from his eyes.

'If anything happens to me I'll say it's your grandmother's

tubers,' he tried a laugh.

In the afternoon, after they had eaten eggs and liver, they drove to the kopjie. He parked the car and they found a jutting rock at the edge of a steep slope, to sit on. The whole city was laid out below and around them. It had just rained and the air and the earth smelt damp. He planted her on his knees, opened her a quart and put his ear to her breasts and said, 'Merry Christmas, Fatima.'

When he left her at the bus terminus and hit the highway the sun was setting.

He put on jazz music and cruised along at a hundred kilometres an hour. He seldom drove faster than that. The car was his friend. She knew his journeys, his haunts, his deepest secrets. She understood his moods. She almost knew his thoughts. He never wanted to punish her by driving her too hard. He liked driving alone, at night, just him and the car, the music and the strong beam of light slicing through the dark. It helped him to reflect on himself, and take stock of his life. Distance made him think of the past and the future, of things that had to be done.

Tonight, for a Christmas Eve, the road seemed empty. He passed very few cars. He drove through that the part of the country which he loved best, rolling farmland, bound by hills on the horizon. Normally, by Christmas, the fields would be awash with knee-high maize, cotton, soya beans and tobacco, but most were over-grown with weeds. The huge dairy farms had been partitioned off among the new settlers and a lot of the plots lay fallow. In the dusk, little fires glowed from the pole and dagga huts.

Reform had its price.

He stopped at the first town to buy some beer. At the garage, two dogs, one black, one brown, rushed up to lick his hands and wag their tails around his shins. He beat them off with empty bottles, but they led him into the kiosk, and waited outside. When he came out again, they led him back to the car.

He drove on for another half hour; then stopped at another garage to relieve himself. Two more dogs, one black, the other brown, appeared out of the grass and led him to the door of the toilet and back to the car. He beat them off. Back on the road, a single strong yellow light appeared behind him, approaching him fast, like a one-eyed truck and he pulled to the side to let it overtake him. Suddenly the light behind went out, only to appear in front of him, travelling in the same direction. Around a curve the light disappeared, but when the road straightened out the light reappeared, this time coming towards him. Two animals, a black and a brown dog, crossed his beam and ran into the grass so that he had to brake sharply to avoid hitting them. The approaching light vanished.

He pulled off again, glancing behind him and ahead. He thought perhaps it was car-jackers stalking him and he stepped hard on the accelerator. He switched off the radio and checked the doors. He was surprised there were no roadblocks all the way and for a moment he thought he had taken a wrong turn out of the highway. He drove until the boot and windows rattled and the accelerator nosed on 140 k.p.h. The lights of Kadoma leapt into view. He slowed down as he entered it. The road was lit and there were a few cars parked on the road-sides. A night club was open and he could hear the noise of the music and the talking. He parked the car outside the club, but as he was locking up the two dogs appeared, licking his boots and brushing his knees with their tails. This time he did not beat them off. He was too stunned. They led him to the entrance of the club and vanished into an alley.

He entered the night-club. Everyone was laughing and shouting. A man he did not know called out his name and he raised his hand in salute and proceeded to the toilet. He splashed cold water over his head and face; wiped his glasses, went back to the bar and ordered a beer. He felt secure here, in the crowd, but he did not want to join the merriment. A young woman drinking a Fanta smiled at him and he went across and said to her, 'I'm driving *kumusha* for Christmas. Can you come with me, to keep me company? It's about two hours away.'

She said at once, 'All right. Take me home so that I can change first.'

She went with him to the car. At the entrance he looked around him for the dogs but they did not appear. She showed him to her place, a tiny room in a cottage with a roof shaped like an elephant's back. She went behind her wardrobe and changed into a white blouse and red skirt; threw combs, Vaseline, a bar of soap, a toothbrush, toothpaste and lipstick into her black handbag and was ready.

In the car she did not talk. She sat on the back seat. Once or twice he switched on the passenger light inside the car to make sure she was still there and look at her face: she only smiled back at him. He offered her a beer but she shook her head. They drove for some time, till he suddenly began to feel sleepy. He pulled into a lay-by and said to her, 'Can I rest for a little bit?' She nodded and he reclined his seat.

When he woke up it was six o'clock and the sun had just risen. The road was deserted. She was sitting at the back, watching over him as if she had not slept. 'Merry Christmas,' he said, and she smiled. He got her a plastic container of water from the boot and she washed her face and brushed her teeth and fixed her face. He ran water over his head and face; then they were off.

When they arrived in Gweru, the city was still asleep. He did not see anyone, not even milkmen or bread vendors. His heart fluttered when they approached the final garage and the turn off to the Chari plot; and felt his recognition of the mournful *muunga* trees lining the road and the old primary school, now overgrown with grass, which his sisters had attended. While their parents were still alive the family had gathered here, almost ritualistically, three times a year, but now only he and Garai had come once in twenty months.

At the turn off to the plot, the car ran on, as if with a mind of its own, straight past the junction towards the city. It turned to the right, avoiding the market place and the milling company and continued through the industrial sites, past the bakery and the police residential quarters, past the abattoir and the medical centre to the cemetery.

The car stopped under the ageless pafa tree and he felt himself alight from it, and go through the gap in the hedge, into the maze of tombstones. He heard himself trudge to the centre, towards a tombstone shaped like an open Bible and flanked by two mounds of earth. He felt himself fall on his knees into the soft damp earth as he hugged, first the bible-shaped stone, and then each of the two mounds of earth. He rose to his feet and stood there with a bowed head for some moments, then walked back to the car.

The woman was still sitting in the car, watching him. He started his vehicle and drove back to the city. At the market place he gave her some money and she found a bus to take her home, back to where he had picked her up. The bus was full and she had to stand in the aisle. He waited till the bus pulled out of the terminus; then waved.

She waved back and smiled.

At a garage near the market place he found a toilet and washed the brown soil off his jeans and his body. On the way to the plot he took his foot off the accelerator and the car moved on its own. It was as if it knew where it was going. At the gate of the old house children ran to meet him; his children, Garai's children, his sister's children, the lodgers' children. They surrounded the car and cheered loudly.

Veronica and Maiguru Mai Emily were at the tap, cleaning tripe and intestines. Tindo, Bertha and Kata came out in their aprons, holding pots and brooms. In the yard Garai, Shepherd and Kata's husband Maneto were in their overalls, chopping up the pink carcase of the ox, which lay on its back with legs in the air.

'Dad, dad,' said Ticha, 'We thought you'd died in an accident.'

'We reported you to the police as a missing person,' Garai said, wiping his nose with a bloody hand.

He got out of the car and leaned on the side of the bonnet.

'I had a strange journey,' he began, but did not know how to continue.

Veronica turned back to the tap. Maiguru Mai Emily put her hands on his arm and wept. Garai cocked his ears skeptically.

**

Later on several people would tell him that the black dog and brown dog were guardian ancestral spirits guiding him home.

10

S isi Maud comes to see him in the morning. Mike Tyson's cousin allows him to go out and talk to her in the park, under the trees. She hugs him very tight, holds his face in her long slim hands and kisses him on the mouth. She is a tall woman with a firm, generous body that has almost recovered from early motherhood. She hands him a book she has brought him to read. He repeatedly assures her that he is OK. She hugs him the way she did when he surprised her in her office, just days before he flew off to the States.

Then, he had taken her out for a farewell drink at an inn on one of the nearby farms and they had sat on the rocks under the blue sky and eaten roasted *matumbu*, while gossiping mischievously about their old school teachers, singing old Dutch Reformed Church songs and chatting about everything under the sun. That day he had felt a premonition of his impending loneliness and she had promised to write to him. And write to him she did – later. Long rambling e-mails, but razor sharp and deliciously wicked in the detail – sisterly jokes – but she always she asked about his wife and children.

Sisi Maud is a widow. Her husband had died almost five years previously from cancer. She initially took his death badly, but has mended well. Her last child is at university, her career is blossoming and now the world is beckoning to her. She is nursing startling new fantasies.

She understands his plight as only someone raised as an orphan can. Like him, she believes in survival and secrecy. She has carefully guarded her health and sanity, while carving a niche for herself in this cruel country, and he envies her that. She is worried by his reckless mirth and his inability to believe in himself, but cannot lecture him about his life.

He cannot take her into the annexe to introduce her to its inmates and she respects that. She scarcely knows about the other annexes in his life – he doubts if anyone does – and he sometimes thinks she is a little naïve not see beyond what he tells her.

He wants to get out of this place and go out with her and be free to partake again of life, and celebrate friendship.

***

Gogo Magirazi pushes her biscuit-size spectacles against the bridge of her nose, ties up her gown and says, 'She did not sleep. She had three attacks and was talking to herself all night.'

'Is she always like this?' he asks.

'Whenever that friend of hers comes to visit her, she gets worse. I don't know what poison she brings her, but maybe the nurses ought to stop her coming.'

'But what is her problem, Gogo?'

'What's her problem? How should I know? Do you understand your problem? All I know is when they first brought her here she had just tried to kill herself by swallowing a whole bottle of pills.'

The inmates are quiet after breakfast and their morning's medication, and are stretched out drowsily on chairs. It must be the hot sun and the pills. And the milk. There is a new patient in prison garb and handcuffs brought in the previous day by the police. He is kicking, struggling and lowing like a young bull being castrated. They say he murdered his father after he caught the latter sleeping with his wife and has been violent ever since. They locked him in the dark room upstairs. This is where the new arrivals are initially housed, before being promoted to the dorms

– he remembers his own first night there.

Murdering your father! People are doing crazy things these days; sleeping with their son's wives or with their daughters or sisters, in order for their businesses to thrive, or to rid themselves, so they believe, of evil spirits or cure themselves of AIDS. Women with barren wombs are stealing babies to appease their complaining husbands. He has even read an article about four women who'd kidnapped a man and taken turns to rape him, leaving him naked in a bush with the note, 'Congratulations. Now we have given you AIDS.'

Then there was that mortician who calmly sawed a frozen body into neat sections and dumped them, one by one, night after night, at strategic spots in the Avenues. Street kids found one of the chunks and almost barbecued it, thinking it was pork …

***

There is no one to talk to. Mr Pimples has assumed a sour, begrudging look. Did he perhaps want to be elected chairman? Does he have relapses, or turn violent? Are his stories about the board-room fights true or imagined? What about his claims of ancestral warnings, and his crusade against milk? Who brings him scented soap, deodorant, towels, toothpaste, and money for newspapers and cigarettes when nobody comes to visit him? How long has he been here?

Yesterday, Farai tried to talk to Do-You-Know-Me? She answered in monosyllables or by nodding her head. She is in Form 3 at a boarding school in the Eastern Highlands. Sometimes she sits in the garden, reading her textbooks while Hypotenuse puts aside her exercise books and helps the girl with her maths. She is obviously a bright child. Whatever could have happened to turn her into a zombie?

Hypotenuse behaves as if nothing had happened between herself and Farai on that first afternoon, in the sitting room, on the seats in front of the TV, when he was an astronaut streaking towards

Zobus and she slipped her hand in his pyjamas and made him wet. Perhaps she took advantage of him because he was new. Or perhaps nothing really happened. But sometimes he thinks she looks at him with eyes that want to tell him something he cannot fathom. She never stops working in her exercise books unless she is eating or dozing. Maybe her dreams are filled with the rhombus of her ambitions and the quadratic equation of her failures. Perhaps her husband left her when she started to behave like this. Perhaps she is a freak and enjoys doing what she did to him. Maybe she is a teacher or even a lecturer in a college.

Perhaps she is like that junior school-teacher in the papers who punished her disobedient pupils by making them suck her tits ...

Farai wants to talk to the inmates and find out about them. After all they voted for him and he is now their chairman. He must know about each one of them. And, as chairman, he must follow up on the proposals he made at the meeting. There are still a handful of people who he has not talked to, beyond exchanging one or two sentences. There is a man who cracks his knuckles and spits into a khaki handkerchief whenever Farai approaches. And another who always eats his food out of his shoes. He has not seen them change, or noted any improvements in their condition. Some people walk with slouching gaits and refuse to be talked to most of the time.

Several nights, after lights out when the inmates are in bed, he sneaks back to talk to Sister Nondo, the night nurse. Now she lets him into the office and he sits with her, warming himself at the heater. The slim doctor does not mind him. After all, he is the chairman, and an annexe chairmen can be allowed a few small privileges. The slim 'doctor' is supplementing his O-levels and he asks him if he can bring his essays and summaries so that he can read them for him and Farai agrees. He promises to find him a copy of one of his textbooks. You scratch my back and I'll scratch yours, after all.

'Sister Nondo, when do you think they will let me go home?' he asks.

'Any day now,' she says.

He knows they're watching him to see if he is well enough to be trusted to go home, so he puts on his best behaviour. Yesterday the psychiatrists were delayed at the main hospital and missed their visit.

'Do you think I'm OK now, Sister?'

'Almost. I wouldn't trust you into this office if I didn't think you were. You recovered in record time. Some people take months, even years, to get to where you are now.'

He knows he must not seem too anxious, but says, 'But do you think I'll ever be really well again, Sister?'

'Who's ever really OK? Think of all the people with high blood pressure, recurrent migraine, asthma, diabetes, ulcers, cancer, amnesia, TB or AIDS. People who are blind, deaf, dumb or disabled. Siamese twins, or children with hearts or brains full of water ... You are just one among hundreds of millions of so-called 'sick' people. You should count yourself lucky. You can see, hear, eat, walk, think, work and look after yourself. All you have to do is take a few pills a day.'

He nods. He wants to tell her that somebody said that everyone was mad; or that, as Mr Pimples said, everyone is a fool. He wants to tell her that there are some ailments that medicine cannot heal.

He knows Sister Nondo enjoys chatting to him. She has finished his novel, and is now half way into a thick Barbara Cartland paperback. Perhaps she spends half her nights reading. Perhaps she, like him, is facing a void in her life, and so substitutes literature for an empty reality. When she summarises a book, he can tell that she has a good grasp of plot, characters and issues. He wants to ask her but his mind is working in low gear. Ideas sink like sediment to the bottom of his brain and he has to return to basics.

'Are you married, Sister Nondo?' he ventures, eventually.

'I don't know.'

'How is that?'

'Well, there's a man I loved who gave me a baby. You know how it is with nurses, with our night shifts and all that. Our jobs are anti-social and we are quick to accept men who pay us reasonable attention. He was good to me and I thought he loved me. He was a bookkeeper in a shoe factory.I introduced him to my family. His prospects were good and he was studying for CIS. But his factory closed down and he was retrenched. When he lost his job he lived with me. I had two rooms in Highfield. I was already pregnant then. I bought him food, clothes … everything, even beer. He lived off me. Literally. He looked for another job but couldn't find anything. Then he got a visa for Britain to train as a male nurse. The Britain brigade, you know. Pounds. He said he would send for me and the baby once he'd settled down. I helped him raise the money for his airfare and accompanied him to the airport. That was the last time I saw him. He never wrote back to say where he was, or what he was doing. He didn't send anything. His sisters knew where he was, but they wouldn't tell me. When I gave birth, his sisters came to the hospital to see me and later I gave them photos of the baby. Then they too stopped seeing me. I heard through the grapevine that he was not studying to be a nurse, but working odd jobs, cleaning fish, looking after old people and packing things on supermarket shelves. That's when I decided to cancel him out of my life.'

So I'm not the only person who was let down or let somebody down, Farai reflects, and asks, 'But have you considered going to Britain to work there, yourself? You are a trained nurse and Zimbabwean nurses are in demand.'

'Me, go to Britain? To work twelve hours a day? Have you seen the queues for visas at the embassy? I'd have to think about it. It's not easy to raise a child out there. My baby comes first. And besides, if we all leave who is going to look after *sascams* like you?'

I think he's a nice man. I like him very much. He's cheerful, funny, intelligent and sociable. He can converse about anything – you never know what he'll say next. He's a good listener. I enjoyed his book very much. I like the way he sneaks in to chat me up in the evenings when the other inmates are asleep. I wonder what he was like before he cracked. Was his disorder latent all along, and something triggered it off? He's very strong and and has pulled through quickly but does he know he'll never be the same? Will he ever understand himself? Will his wife understand him? I wonder what kind of woman she is. I obviously can't ask him about her without seeming interested, or indiscreet. She seemed rather aloof when she brought him toiletries and fresh pyjamas. I wouldn't mind being friends with him after he's discharged; he says he will bring more of his books. He's obviously a bit of a flirt but I don't mind that. He's great company. As a woman, I'm charmed, but judging by what his wife and the doctors have said, he must be very difficult to live with.

***

He is discharged the next day, after spending exactly a week at the annexe. His two doctors study his cards and comment on his eye contact and gait; the matron is there to vouch for his deportment in the ward. They lecture him about the importance of taking his pills every day, getting enough sleep and having a regular check up – and, of course, on the hazards of alcohol.

The matron goes with him to announce the news to the day nurse. She congratulates him and returns his few belongings. His jeans feel rough and scratchy, his T-shirt is creased and smelly with sweat. His purse bulges with miscellanies that now seem insignificant – Veronica had earlier removed his ID and cards and anything she deemed important and God knows what she had discovered thereby.

The day nurse gives him the phone so that he can tell his news to Veronica, and ask her to pick him up. She says she will come at once.

The chairman asks to meet his committee to bid them farewell and they are summoned to the lounge. Peter Ndlovu comes first, hugging his football under his arm. Taxi-driver follows, thoughtfully scratching the gash on his head. Miss Fits is fetched from the dorm, and hurries in with her slapping slippers and crossword puzzles, extinguishing a half-finished cigarette in an empty cigarette box.

'Maybe we should call in everybody,' he suggests, and the day nurse goes out to the garden to call in all the patients. They troop in and surround him with envious smiles. He is sad to leave them, sorry to part with his comrades who have made this place his home for the past week.

'I have been discharged,' he tells them. 'I want to say goodbye.' Goodbyes are difficult.

He sees now that the elections were a charade, an attempt to give this mediocre place a weak semblance of that clawing world out there. Even if he had stayed for months, how much could he have changed things, he wonders.

'Maybe we should all contribute some money to buy our chairman a card and some flowers,' Peter Ndlovu suggests.

'We can organise that later,' says the day nurse.

'And now we will have to hold new elections,' says Mr Pimples. 'Maybe we should make it a requirement that only long-staying patients be elected to the committee.'

'We'll talk about that later, at the next meeting,' says the day nurse.

Mazitulela swallows and half raises his hand. He wants to say something, a prayer, maybe.

Then Miss Fits has an idea. She rushes out to the garden and gathers bougainvillea bracts from the hedge, arranges them into a small bouquet and, with a suitable bow, hands them to the chairman. The chairman accepts the flowers and there is applause.

'You are supposed to give your secretary a hug, I think,' says Miss Fits, laughing, holding out her arms.

'That's right,' says the nurse. Farai puts his arms round Miss Fits' waist and embraces her closely.

'Don't I get a hug, too?' says Hypotenuse. 'I'm also a woman.'

He hugs all the women, including the nurse, and shakes hands with the men. Mr Pimples hits his elbows with his hands and says, 'Way to go, chairman.'

There is a knock. Mike Tyson's cousin opens the door and Veronica enters. She is surprised to see the crowd at the office.

'This is my wife,' the chairman says, and they all say, 'Hello,' and she says 'Hello' back.

'I am your *babamukuru*,' Mr Pimples says, stepping forward and shaking Veronica's hand. 'Please look after my brother well. '

The chairman has an idea. He digs into his paper bags and holds out what is left of his toiletries. There is a surge forward and arms reach out. John White grabs the bottle of Vaseline, Do-you-know-me? deftly secures the tube of toothpaste. Mazitulela picks up the fallen bar of soap from the floor but, deferring to age, hands it over to Gogo Magirazi.

Farai has to go. He feels almost sad to leave. This ward has been his home for a week, and the inmates have become his family. He is glad to be returning home and yet, if he is honest, he is also scared of the world out there. Clutching the small bouquet and the plastic bags he follows Veronica out to the park, to the car. The blue Corolla waits serenely in the shade, under the trees. She opens the door and he gets in beside her. She reverses out of the park, out of the gates.

'I'll go and drop you at home,' she says matter of factly. 'I have a meeting at two o'clock.'

***

At the house, Maria the maid and Thomas the gardener come to the car to greet him.

'*Makadii* Daddy?'

'*Maakunzwa sei*, Daddy?'

Thomas goes back to the swimming pool and Maria takes the paper bags stuffed with his few possessions from him. Veronica backs out of the gate.

In the lounge there is a large bouquet and a colourful Welcome Home card signed by Veronica and the children. The hi-fi is tuned to Radio Zimbabwe and a popular female DJ is reading listeners' greetings and playing songs.

He pauses to look at the pictures of his mother and his children on the mantelpiece then proceeds to the bedroom. He opens the wardrobes. His clothes hang neatly on the rails. Above them, on the top shelf, there is the pile of files and envelopes and the lunch box full of old bank books and receipts, undisturbed. He opens Veronica's wardrobe – all her dresses appear to be there. His books are on the left side of the headboard, hers on the right.

He switches on the boom box on his side of the bed and B.B. King croons, on tape:

Hold on

I'm nothing without you

What do you do when you come back home from the annexe, in the afternoon?

In the study, there is a pile of letters, a large, hand-delivered envelope, and a whole page of telephone messages. He riffles through the letters, piling them on one side of the table and throwing the crumpled up envelopes into a bin. There are five telephone messages from one person, his editor Georgina, asking him to call him back. He picks up the phone and listens. Miraculously, there is a dial tone now. He dials a number.

'Georgina?'

'Farai! Where on earth have you been? I've been looking for you all over the place. I called your house three or four times and was told you were not there. Are you OK?'

'I'm fine. I'm fine,' he says.

Georgina is a slim white woman with curly auburn hair and piercing brown eyes. She has a razor sharp eye for detail and a keen vision for books, for literature. She is more than a professional colleague – a friend. She definitely senses that something is amiss, that this is not just another one of his disappearing acts, but is prudent enough not to ask too much. He wonders what their maid, Maria, told her about his whereabouts; what alibi, if any, Veronica cooked to cover up for his absence. He decides not to explain.

'I'm fine,' he tells her. 'And thank you for the page proofs you sent me. I'll quickly look at them and get them back to you.'

'The typesetter wanted them this week, but if you are tied up I can ring her up and ask for an extension.'

Maria taps on the door and kneels down to announce that lunch is ready. He sits down, alone, at the large table in the dining room, to eat sadza, butternut, sweet cabbage and nuggets of brisket which is the usual home fare. While he is eating, Sharai and Ticha return from school, dropped off by his neighbour Baba Jane. The children shake hands with him, awkwardly. Ticha says, 'Good afternoon, Daddy,' and Sharai says, 'How are you?'

After eating, he samples the first few pages of the page proofs but cannot concentrate. The stories read as if they'd been written by someone else. He is trapped by his own words. He decides to leave them until the next day.

When Veronica comes home at six she finds him watching TV with the children. She smiles and says, *'Kanjani? Waswera?'* and goes to the kitchen to help Maria prepare rice with peanut butter and bream. He remembers to take his nightly pills before eating. Veronica serves him and sits on the sofa next to him, eating. Before the news is over he is already dozing and he goes to sleep. The bed feels strangely large after the small, single ones at the annexe.

When Veronica comes in he is already fast asleep, snoring. She covers him up with the blankets.

***

He wakes up late the next morning, reluctant to get out of bed, and he realises now why at the annexe they were made to get up early and go to bed early. Early to bed and early to rise. While strolling in the yard, inspecting the garden, he sees his neighbour Mai Jane hanging up the washing. He goes to the fence and greets her.

'I'm sorry I caused you trouble,' her says to her.

'Trouble? What trouble, Mr Chari? There's nothing to talk about.'

How does one begin to talk about it all, to retrace events and apologise? Is it even necessary to apologise? Must he call Mai Tapiwa, his other neighbour, or Mainini Goto, or Veronica's parents and sisters, or his own sisters, or Veronica's boss, or Wilbert? To say what? Hadn't enough damage been caused already? Hadn't he in that short, terrible tangle of days stripped himself bare for all to see?

'Don't phone anybody,' Wilbert advises him. 'Just carry on as if nothing unusual happened. You're out of the woods already.'

Soon after that, Sekuru Tumai phones to remind him that whenever he feels well enough, he should accompany him to the Eastern Highlands to seek the services of a spiritual healer. Playing for time, Farai replies that he will not forget to do so.

Then there is the question of visitors. What happens if a stream of them come to see him, asking questions, unsettling and exhausting him. How will he deal with the curious coming merely to encounter him, a returnee from the annexe. How can he remain in the closet, if half the city has already enjoyed the gossip and the rumours?

Clara advises that visitors be kept to a minimum, or barred altogether and that Veronica deal directly with their inquiries. So, during the afternoon, when Veronica phones home to ask if her prayer group, of which she is cell leader, can have their pre-arranged monthly meeting at the house, he says, thoughtfully, 'Maybe next month.'

Normally when the group holds prayers at his house, he flees to the pub, but once or twice, when he was not fast enough with the car or garage keys and they trekked in before he could leave, he has had to join them. They are nearly all women in their thirties and early forties – middle class – with one or two men hitched along. Sometimes a pastor comes with them. Some of them are widows or divorcees. Their eyes are bright with the Word and their skins glow with clean living. They sing wonderful Pentecostal songs and pray in a babel of tongues. They turn otherwise mundane incidents, both personal and impersonal – into fantastic testimonies. They drink tea, eat biscuits and sell each other mushrooms, peanut butter, eggs and sweaters, while trading news of promotions and investments. And, of course, they pay the church tithe.

He knows they have heard about his case and want to pray for him tonight but he tells Veronica 'no'. He knows they are knocking at his door and denies them entry.

What is it he so distrusts about them? Aren't they his wife's best friends? He, who was raised as a God-fearing, Dutch Reformed boy? Didn't he feed from the same Bible; suckle from the same tunes, dread the same Gehenna? Or is Gehenna something in the individual's mind? Was his recent experience merely a test run? Has he banished from memory all the grim history of his family and, unlike Sekuru Tumai, killed any belief in the spiritual and supernatural world? Or is it that he abhors anyone who harbours cast-iron beliefs and abdicates all responsiblity to God?

Where shall he find help? Does he think he needs help?

***

I am a survivor. I was in and out of there in record time. Just a week. I was never really 'mad'. I only broke down from stress. After all, madness is relative. It's a concept created by Victorians and die-hard traditionalists. People with a very narrow view of things. Those people outside annexes are just as 'mad' as those within, perhaps even 'madder'! Society is one big chauvinist towards the 'unwell'.

Bloody twits! Borrowing from me left to right and centre and then procrastinating or refusing altogether to pay me back. Treating me as if I were Father Christmas. Borrowing from my very soul. Holding back and pushing me to the forefront to sort our family problems and blaming me when things go wrong. Berating me even when I'm sick. Plastering me up with labels. Farai this, Farai that. Prevaricating over my fate. None of you has any idea what I went through; no clue what I intend to make of my experience. Just you wait.

At the annexe I grew up. Look, I stared death squarely in the face. I learnt to treasure every ounce of good health; to savour every minute of life; tuck in my long tail, as wise old father baboon is supposed to do, and just listen to friends, siblings, spouses and relatives. I learned to switch off and reflect, and sometimes just let the world go by.

I stopped moaning ages ago. I said, hell, this has happened and so what? Ancestors or coincidence, sunshine or ill winds, bones or bibles, science or fate, I've got to get on with my life. I don't give a damn about tradition or so-called modernity – what a simplistic way to look at life! If God, my ancestors or fate are on my side, well and good, I'll welcome them on board.

I will be ME, and I'll live, I'll love, I'll laugh.

11

isi Maud and Georgina invite him for lunch. The two women are mutual friends. They sit in a garden in a respectable restaurant in the avenues.

'We haven't done this in a long time,' says Georgina, brushing her curls. 'Drinks?'

Sisi Maud studies the drinks menu.

'How about some white wine, Maud? Yes? And Farai, what will you have? A beer?'

'Just a cold glass of hydrogen oxide,' he says.

'What's that?' says Georgina.

'He's showing off the little chemistry he still remembers from three decades ago,' Sisi Maud quips.

'When we used to write home to our fathers to send us more money for photosynthesis,' he adds.

'Just be sure not to poison yourself, or we wouldn't know what to tell Veronica, especially since you've been back only two weeks,' says Georgina. 'How is she?'

'Fine.'

'She must be so happy you are back. ... I wonder what she thinks about the current scandals in the investment houses and the banking sector?'

'Well, I don't know. She never talks about them.'

'I just hope she doesn't get caught up in the rot,' says Sisi Maud.

Farai feels his body rocking steadily towards the table. He smiles weakly. He is happy to be surrounded by friends and the sun is warm. The waiters in starched whites glide from table to table, with drinks and silver platters of food. Theirs is the only racially mixed group. The people on the other tables are either all white, or all black; still separated, twenty years into independence. Middle-class patrons, with an obvious sprinkling of business people or the strayed bureaucrat. Sisi Maud of farm bottle stores and barbecued *matumbu* has obviously chosen this place as a compromise, to make Georgina comfortable.

The two women order a bottle of white wine.

'Are you sure you don't want a beer, Farai?' Georgina asks again, lighting a cigarette. 'Just one?'

'I have to finish reading your page proofs tonight, remember,' Farai says. Sisi Maud looks aside and caresses her bangles. She knows.

'Oh wow! I'm impressed,' Georgina teases him.

'My muse stayed up late last night and is taking a rather long siesta,' Farai responds.

The waiter pours a little wine in a glass and gives it to Georgina to taste. Georgina, the white woman.

'No, give it to Maud,' says Georgina. 'She's our designated wine taster.'

Sisi Maud approves the wine and they order food. Sisi Maud orders trout, Georgina a tuna fish salad and Farai his usual, a large T-bone steak. He is amazed at how he always orders the same food in restaurants, as if he is afraid to experiment with menus. Afraid to experiment with alternatives.

The food is some time coming. While they are waiting Farai suddenly remembers his afternoon pills and he goes to the toilet to take them.

'That was a very quick trip,' says Sisi Maud.

'I can go again if you want.'

They gossip, inevitably, about books, book reviews and publishing. Sisi Maud talks about new arts projects for women. Georgina talks with distaste against the restrictions on the media and hate speech.

Sisi Maud leans back in her chair, nods slowly and kneads the table with her fingers.

The conversation slips slowly to cats and dogs rescued from hastily abandoned farms and dispossessed white farmers trooping in to seek refuge with friends in the suburbs. The land question looms, like a shadow, over the table.

Farai feels his medicine melt inside him and seep up from the bottom of his belly to his throat, causing the creep of nausea that he is starting to get used to. He says little and attacks the edges of his steak with his knife. He recalls a ridiculous article in one of the partisan papers falsely crediting him with the 'heroic' act of manhandling and removing from the stage a fellow countryman and writer accused of having spoken disparagingly about his nation at a workshop away from home. To begin with, he, Farai, had never been to the workshop, or even been out of the country at the time. The fictitious story spread from one paper to another, from one eager mouth to the next. And in the streets some people scowled, and others stopped him and shook his hand and said, 'Well done. You did what everybody was afraid to do.'

Talk about newspapers! Making fools of every one, like that.

He decided it was not worth his time or dignity to respond or to or sue the paper, and kept people guessing.

After all, he is not one to flaunt his opinion on contentious issues.

And so they eat and talk, and talk and eat and drink, three friends united by a common love of stories, of laughter, and books. Sisi Maud knows, or believes she knows. Georgina will begin to suspect, will know, later. He cannot fool her, or anyone, forever.

This lunch is his first effort to drag himself up out of the stiff mud of his recent past and slip back into the waters of his element.

***

Garai's graduation party is a success.

First they all go to see him capped in the University Great Hall and assemble for the photos, then in the afternoon they drive out to his house at the research station for the party.

Their father, while alive, had made it his principle to stare misfortune in the face and quickly supplant it with merriment and celebration. If there was any one principle of his father's that Garai had adopted absolutely, it was this. Success, setback, growth, ran the family credo. Yet Garai had been at loggerheads many times with his father, half his life perhaps, while he was so much like his father now – the way parents and their children so often perfectly contradict and complement each other like two sides of the same coin.

And so Farai walks out of the annexe straight into his brother's graduation party, in a juxtaposition that would shame the inscrutable forces of malevolence. He steps into the presence of a capped and gowned, exuberant Garai, stone cold sober.

'*Hes* Blaz.'

'*Hes* Blaz.'

'Had a good trip?'

'Yes. Everything going well?'

'Oh, yes.'

He notices, as if for the first time, how Garai looks so much like him, just a tiny bit shorter, with a lighter skin and a more generous pot-belly. Their voices have the same timbre.

Siblings.

'Want a beer? Oh, maybe not. Guys! Guys, listen. This is my brother Farai, the one who comes after me. *Buda ndibudewo.*'

The men are sitting in chairs or on stools, or squatting, drinking round a huge bonfire in the middle of the yard and he goes around shaking hands with each of them. He, the young brother of their director, the new doctor of plants. He, the one who writes books. And how many of them know already where he's been, just a week ago? Some of them he knows from the research farm, others are friends, neighbours, relatives – Sekuru Tumai rises from his chair to hug him. Shepherd offers him a chair but he has to go into the house first, to greet the women.

Everyone is there who could be there; his sisters, Maiguru Mai Emily, Veronica's sisters, Garai's in-laws, a childhood aunt and some of his late mother's associates from the hometown; fussing and sweating over great big pots of rice, beef and chicken. Children scream and yelp, chasing each other and scurrying in and out of the house.

'*Makadi*i Babamunini?'

'*Makadii* Sekuru?'

'*Wakadii munin'ina?*'

Outside men are roasting meat and sausages over the fire and the disco is playing an Alick Macheso album. There are coloured lights in the trees and someone flashes a camera in his face. A sweet oily aroma hangs in the air. Garai leans over to snatch up a rope of sizzling meat and the front of his gown almost catches in the flame and somebody says, 'Watch out, Doc!' The beers are in a big zinc bath filled with ice. The meat is forked onto waiting plates as soon is it ready, stripped up by bare hands and passed around. Someone brings arm-sized bags of peanuts and roasts them in a pan. Another brings a dish of fried *majuru*. The men are dressed in denims or khakis, shorts, workshop boots and farmer's shoes so that it is difficult to tell who is who. This is another world here, where men are equals wedded to the red soil and happiness is a fire, meat and drink, and your neighbour's ear is open to your triumphs and your woes.

But this is only the appetiser. The women are coming out with big plates of food: there are pots of pumpkin leaf in peanut butter sauce and spiced *madora* and *mazondo* for the initiated.

'You are not eating, Muzukuru,' Sekuru Tumai says to Farai, piling food onto his plate. 'Did you eat well in the States? Who cooked for you?'

The speeches start.

'He's a humble director,' says one speaker.

'He's dedicated to his job,' says another.

'He is fair to everyone.'

'Speech, speech, doctor!' they chorus.

Garai gives a brief speech. He narrates why and how he studied for his Ph.D. He thanks his wife and children for putting up with him in all these years. He thanks the people working with him for their support and exhorts them to persevere and improve their lot. He thanks every one for coming to the party and by so doing honouring not only him, but the whole Chari family.

Listening to his brother speak, just the way he himself would have spoken, Farai cannot help but glow with pride. But he feels hollow, thinking of the emptiness in his own household.

Sekuru Tumai is itching to say something on this auspicious occasion, to bite his *vazukuru's* ears, as it were, and share a few words of wisdom with them. After Garai's speech he summons Garai, Farai, Kata, Bertha and Tindo into a corner.

'I am so happy to be here at your brother's graduation party,' he begins. 'He has set a good example for you all and your children. The people down under the soil will be happy for this wonderful occasion. I would also like to thank your brother for approaching your in-laws, and ensuring that Mai Rumbi returned to your house, Farai, when you were at the annexe. You'll never find another brother like that. For you, Farai, I have three words of advice. One, thank your brother for getting your wife back. Two, respect and look after her, and your family. Three, stop drinking. For all of you, I have this to say. Open your eyes. Look at how things have happened in this family. Look at the way we lost your mother, father and especially your brother Dzimai: cancer, stroke, schizophrenia. Their deaths were too close together and not natural I'd say. I'll say it again, I am not happy with the way our close family have died.'

'What are you suggesting, Sekuru?' Garai asks, pointedly.

'Can't you see there is a pattern emerging? That there is something serious that needs to be attended to? Think of the coincidences! In Farai's case, for instance, that he should have bumped straight into me at the garage after he'd put his car in for repair. I hadn't seen him for years and didn't even know we lived so near each other! Or that his best friend's wife should have pitched up when he was most desperate. Or the brown and black dogs that followed him that Christmas. Can't you see there was a force guiding and protecting him all the time, and that force should be claimed and acknowledged.'

'OK, OK, Sekuru. Do you know who can help us out of this quandary?'

'We can each ask around about various diviners, and compare notes. I'm prepared to accompany you to some people, to introduce you to them, if you want.'

Kata pulls in her legs and draws circles on the ground with a twig. She married into a family that knows about the spirit world, about appeasement rites – people who take the necessary precautions to keep ill-fortune at bay. Bertha, her head in her hands, gazes at the fire in a detached way. Tindo has a youthful eagerness for possibilities. Garai has gradually, after twenty years of phenobarbitone, given in to the rule of science and logic. Farai, the fence sitter, is prepared to hide behind his father's undying maxim, 'Don't entangle yourselves in matters you don't understand.' He is swayed by Sekuru Tumai's views, but being something of a cynic, not wholly convinced.

'Perhaps you want to think about it and talk about it among yourselves, and then come back to me.

Sekuru Tumai is the lonely advocate of the spiritis, outvoted by silence.

***

Such a wonderful, educated man, but so helpless. They're all beautifully educated but still naked to evil winds. Like broiler chickens foraging in the open yard while eagles swoop overhead. Books, books, books. That's all they know. This they don't know, that for black people there is no choice but between the Bible and ancestral spirits. And, maybe, science. No one can idle in neutral gear forever. It's his father's fault, of course, for ditching his real relatives and opting for his workmates and his neighbours in the townships. Totemic relatives, no blood link. So his real relatives conspired to turn the ill winds on his house and his family in order to isolate and punish him. That man saw calamity after calamity. Epilepsy, schizophrenia, cancer, and now this. I said to him 'Mzukuru, can't you see what is happening and what you have to do?' I said 'Go back to your rural home and talk to your blood relatives. Organise a traditional brew and plead with your ancestors to clear the mist and sweep your path for you!' But he said to me, 'No Sekuru Tumai, I'll do no such thing. No child of mine shall ever dabble with the unknown. Let sleeping dogs lie!' Now, tell me, Mzukuru, wherever it is you are, don't you want your children to bring your spirit back from the dead so that you can guard your family? Aren't your elders in the world of the dead, turning their backs on you and saying silently, 'Go back where you came from. You don't belong to the fold. You haven't been reclaimed and cleansed. We don't know you. Didn't you leave children when you were alive?' And, tell me, Mzukuru, how many devout church people did you yourself know of who had ancestral brews prepared for them after they died, with or against their wish? Deacons like

you, prophets, evangelists or even church ministers? Who are you
to spit in the face of your ancestors, and your culture? Now tell
me, Mzukuru, why did Farai crack? Was it stress, drink, or the
chemistry of his brain? Or was it the ill winds, or the sour breath
of wronged ancestors? Tell me, Mzukuru?'

***

Farai stops at the supermarket to buy a sack of oranges and three bunches of bananas. At the gates of the annexe he runs into Mbuya MaSibanda emptying food scraps into the bin and she says to him, '*Hes*, Mhani, Muzukuru. You're driving now! I can see you're OK.' He laughs with her and gives her an orange and a banana.

At the outpatients there is already a long queue winding from the car park into the building. It is a Monday, one of the two days for out-patients.

He leaves the fruit in the car and enters the building. The queue is even longer inside; there are scores more people sitting on the benches, waiting for their turn to see the doctor.

He sees a nurse in white and says to her, 'Excuse me, Sister. I've come for my check up. Am I in the right place?'

The nurse looks at his cards and says, 'Who is your doctor? Are you a patient here?'

'I was discharged a few weeks ago.'

The nurse smiles at him and says, with a pitying but knowing look, 'Discharged? You haven't been discharged. Nobody who is hospitalised here is ever "discharged". Didn't they tell you? You're still a patient – maybe forever. Join the queue.'

He goes to the end of the queue and says to the man who is last, 'Please keep my place, I'll be back soon.'

He takes the oranges and bananas out of the car and goes to the ward. He knocks on the door. Mike Tyson's cousin opens it and says, 'Can I help you?'

~ 171 ~

'Hello,' he says. 'It's me.'

'Oh, it's you! How are you, Mr Chairman?'

'I just came by to say hello. How is everyone?'

'They're fine.'

'Can I come in?'

'You'd have to see the matron, but she's in a meeting right now.'

'What about the day nurse?'

'She's inspecting the wards. What did you want to see them about?'

'Just to say hello.'

'But it's not visiting time yet. Can you come back at one o'clock?'

'I brought these for the patients.' He holds up the bags of fruit.

'You can leave them with me.'

Farai wants to hand over the parcels himself. Mike Tyson's cousin senses this and says, 'Hold on. I'll get the nurse for you.'

The day nurse comes over and says, 'Oh, Mr Chari. How nice to see you. You look well. How are you, Mr Chairman? How are things at home?'

'I'm fine, I'm fine. I just stopped by to say hello. I brought these for my friends in the wards. I hope there is enough for everybody.'

'How thoughtful of you. If you leave the fruit with me I'll make sure they get it.'

'Couldn't I see the patients?'

'It's not visiting time and right now they are busy cleaning up the dorms . Did you want to see anyone in particular?'

'Well, yes and no. How's the committee doing? Do you have a new chairman?'

'We haven't had the elections yet. But you can be sure Mr Rinashe is already campaigning for the post.'

'Mr Rinashe?'

'The man with pimples all over his face. He tried to stick posters all over the walls and I had to stop him.'

'And how is my secretary?'

'Oh, Regina? That girl with epilepsy? She took two half straights of brandy with her medicine and collapsed. She had to be rushed to the main hospital. Apparently somebody was bringing her the alcohol and she was taking it secretly. One day for sure, she will kill herself. Now you will have to let me go, I must attend to the phone.'

'Tell Sister Nondo I forgot about the books but I'll bring them next time I come over,' he says.

At the back of the block he sees Mazitulela's small face squashed against a window pane. She's waving at him and he waves back. He bumps into Sekuru Sithole dragging his hosepipes over the lawn and gives him some money for his tobacco.

The out-patients queue moves slowly. The man at the tail end, keeping his place, is about twenty people from the doors, the queue winding to the consultation rooms is longer still. He decides to wait in the car, and listen to the radio.

The people in the queue are a motley assembly of figures, faces and clothes. They are, of course, almost all black, with a sprinkling of 'coloureds' and two or three whites. Some of the people look deceptively normal. Others have the stooping posture, the stiff gait, upraised arms, and the slow subdued tones that are the trademark of their supposed condition.

It is difficult to believe there are so many people who are suffering from mental or emotional instability and anxiety. They're his comrades singled out from the camouflage of homes, streets, villages, farms and workplaces to receive the salutary little white pills. But he knows there are thousands of others out there, the poor, the 'mad', the forgotten or neglected, who have never taken a pill; people caked black with dirt and matted with lice, given up on or neglected or unfound, daily trampling accustomed streets and footpaths; untiring unsleeping zombies ransacking bins and

garbage heaps and bedding on pavements and alleys and in bur-
rows.

But how come they never get hit by passing cars? Or die of food
poisoning – or do they? Or get bitten by snakes? Do they catch
flue? Pneumonia? Do they ever sleep? Do they dream? And if
they are women, what do they do about their cycles?

And what theatres of horror have they each starred in, the ones
that are lined up here? What scenes of their lives have been shot?
What cameras? What lenses? How have they retraced the steps
back to themselves?

'Hello, Farai.'

'Ah, Hello.'

'How are you?'

'Fine. Fine.'

'Long time no see. Still writing?'

'Ah, yes. And you?'

'Left the teacher's college. Couldn't survive on that. Am now selling cell-phones. Are you in the queue?'

'No. Just waiting for somebody.'

'Me too. My old man. I'll go in and have a look. See you.'

'See you.'

Lies. Lies. Lies. Closets. How does one get out of this closet? Or
is there, in the first place, any closet to hide in?

Out of the car. Into the queue. In through the doors. On the benches. Clutch your cards. Sit. Bury your face between your knees.
Heave forward. Slide your bum. Stop. Bums polishing benches.
Thousands of bums every week. Smoothing the grooves, the
wood.

'Please have your cards ready, *vabereki*.'

Have your cards ready *vabereki*. Like your fare in the combis.
Like your cash at the till, in the shops. Like your IDs at the polls.
Like your papers at the mortuaries.

'And you there Sekuru. Stop walking up and down, *nhaika*. You're blocking the passage.'

In the consultation room the doctor offers him a sweet. She is so casual he doesn't at first believe she is the doctor. And she is so young. Intern, perhaps?

'How are you feeling now? Look me straight in the eye. Are you sleeping well? Eating well? Can you try holding your head up and straightening down your arms when you walk? Are you able to concentrate on your work? It's getting better? Good. I'll reduce your dosage a little so you don't feel sleepy during the day. Come back in a month for another check up. If you find the queues too long here, you can get your own private doctor, but you'd have to pay, of course.'

'Are the drugs available from the pharmacies?'

'Sometimes, and sometimes not. The prices can fluctuate, depending on the suppliers and the exchange rate.'

'And what will happen if this country runs out of foreign currency, doctor? What will you do with people like us?'

'That's a very good question, Mr Chari,' she says and offers him another sweet.

***

At the main hospital the computers are down and the receptionist cannot find out what ward Miss Fits is in without her surname. Someone sends him to Ward C but he does not find her there. Ward D is the paediatric section. He goes through Ward B and when he finally finds her in Ward A, the bell is ringing for visitors to leave.

She is lying in a bed, with bottles, drips and tubes hanging above her. Her eyes are closed and she is so still that she is hardly breathing. She looks small, almost like a child, under the bed cover. He stands over her, gazing at her face, till the woman on the next bed says, 'She hasn't talked since she was brought in two days ago.

She was frothing at the mouth and her breath was rattling as if
something was choking her, but the nurses think she's better now.
Are you her husband?'

'No.'

'Brother, maybe?'

'Just a friend.'

'Nobody has been to see her since she was admitted. Do you think
her people know?'

He takes a peek into her file in a tray at the foot of her bed, but
cannot decipher the doctor's scrawl.

'The nurses won't want to see you looking at the files,' says the
woman again and he realises that the last of the visitors are trooping out of the ward.

He, too, hurries out. 'I'll come back,' he says.

12

Bipolar disorder is a condition that causes unpredictable mood swings and extreme mood shifts. Both males and females experience it.

Bipolar disorders cause dramatic mood swings from overly 'high' and or irritable to sad and hopeless, and then back again, often with periods of normality in-between.

It usually develops during adolescence and childhood. Bipolar disorder is characterised by episodes of depression, mania or mixed depression, which quickly recur causing unnecessary disruption to school, work and social life.

Symptoms of depression include: a persistent sad mood; loss of interest or pleasure in activities that were once enjoyed; significant change in appetite or body weight; difficulty in sleeping or oversleeping; physical slowing or agitation; loss of energy; feelings of worthlessness or inappropriate guilt; difficulty thinking or concentrating; recurrent thoughts of death and suicide.

Mania: abnormally and persistently elevated (high) mood and / or irritability accompanied by at least three of the following symptoms (Four if the mood is merely irritable): overly-inflated self esteem; decreased need for sleep; increased talkativeness; racing thoughts; distractibility; increased goal-directed activity such as shopping; physical agitation; hyper sexuality; excessive involvement in risky behaviours or activities.

Mixed state: Symptoms of mania and depression are present at the same time. The symptom picture frequently includes agitation, trouble sleeping, significant change in appetite, psychosis and suicidal thinking. Depressed mood accompanies manic activation.

***

Veronica probably reads more books about his condition than he himself will ever do. She peruses manuals on alcoholism, boredom, withdrawal, stress, and depression, and writes copious notes. After all, she can converse convincingly with doctors and pharmacists about such diverse subjects as paediatric fevers, ulcers, migraine and allergies. He picks up the books and flips through them. He has settled into his medication regime and his mind is becoming less distracted. He has begun to read again, a few chapters of a book at a time. He makes a preliminary survey of the texts he is supposed to teach in the next academic year, the thought of which makes him anxious. He samples programmes on TV, comedies mostly. He listens to jazz; for him music is the easiest art form to ingest. He consciously works to overcome lethargy, low self-esteem, and feelings of worthlessness; to derive pleasure from simple chores and menial tasks. His doctors warned him that this would take time, and assured him that most of these symptoms would eventually disappear. He knows he should get back as quickly as possible to his old rhythms. Watching Veronica rushing to work, Maria hanging the washing on the line, his children bending over their homework, people clattering about and talking and laughing in the shopping mall and crowds heaving in the streets, he begins to itch for a sense of purpose in his own life. Veronica works hard to resurrect him, to rebuild him. This is her chance to reclaim him. She cooks him his favourite dishes, buys him surprise presents, baths with him; holds him close to her at night. She takes him to movies – once, replete with popcorn, ice-cream and Coke, he falls asleep on her lap, in the theatre. She is silent; she never asks him what he went through and how it began. He wonders why she never asks. And he would so much like to talk to somebody about it so that he can begin to recreate and understand what happened.

They visit Veronica's folks to give their condolences for relatives who died while he was away. Her mother prepares him goat meat and rice with peanut butter. Veronica invites him to a Saturday afternoon braai at her church and finally he agrees to accompany her. They go with the children and sit on the grass, eating sausage roll after sausage roll and drinking Coke after Coke, chatting with her friends, who at once like him. This is as she would want him to be, witty and sociable, the Farai he was when she first met him. She hopes and thinks he is changing, that he will change. She buys him colourful cards with optimistic inscriptions like:

> GOD HAS GREAT PLANS FOR YOU

or:

> DO NOT DESPAIR
> WHEN YOU ARE DOWN AND UNDER
> I SHALL CROWN YOU WITH THE GLORY
> OF MY LOVE

Some of the inscriptions read like poetry, but he discovers with a little disappointment that they are all from the Bible. Secretly, he hopes she does not hope too much. To be honest, he is lukewarm about his spiritual options. He thinks Sekuru Tumai and Veronica are needlessly at loggerheads with each other over his destiny. Sekuru Tumai insists on *hakata*, the diviner's bones, while Veronica believes in prayer. Farai has made up his mind that he will brave the future, just as he hauled himself out of his past.

'What if you had had a breakdown, alone, out there in the States, or it happens again?' Sekuru Tumai urges him. 'Don't you see?'

Farai decides that he will not cancel his lectureship in the USA, and that the sooner he gets back to work the better.

Time is flying. The days are getting shorter. Winter is approaching. He must make the most of the sun because in the north it will be freezing cold.

They go to Great Zimbabwe with the children, for a weekend family holiday. They climb up to the acropolis, stopping at the top to rest, and inspect the cone tower; then he relaxes with Veronica on the cool veranda while the children play netball and swim in the large pool. In the evenings they eat long, elaborate dinners together around a large table, all five of them, listening to soft canned music. After dinner the children go to the room to watch videos and play games while he and she take a walk round the hotel grounds, hand in hand in the moonlight, imbibing the cool night air and the history of the place. He now knows that he should spend more time with his wife, and with his children, in this way. This is his opportunity to change, to re-organise himself and start afresh. He wishes, of course, he had wine, or a beer, to loosen his tongue, so that he can speak freely to Veronica and tell her all the things he has always wanted to, but he knows this might spoil things and decides against it.

In fact, he is not drinking and hardly going out. When Wilbert invites him out once, he only drinks iced water or Coke. He does not talk or laugh as much as he usually does. His cheeks are stiff and his mind distracted by the drugs. Sisi Maud phones him, just to talk. She is too busy with her projects for them to meet. He bumps into her at a workshop, where he is invited to talk on the feasibility and value of teaching creative writing in the country. His paper is well received.

He goes out alone sometimes, but all his friends and acquaintances comment on his sudden reserve. On being asked why he is not drinking, he jokes that he is on a brief 'sabbatical.' Without the heady influence of alcohol, the noise of the pubs seems strident and incongruous, and he leaves early, but he would very much like to be part of it again. One evening, feeling low, he drives alone to an inn on the highway and buys himself a quart of beer. Hadn't the doctor said one or two drinks would be OK? Hesitantly, like a teenager learning to drink, he puts the bottle to his lips. It's amazing how quickly and naturally it all comes back – the half bitter taste of white froth, and the warmth of the lager curling up inside him. Because he has not drunk alcohol for some time, it quickly goes to his head. By the time he has finished the quart, he hears a shrilling noise in his ears and feels a funny light-headedness. He drives home in a slight panic. That night Veronica says mournfully, 'Have you started again? It's your choice.'

He realises that his real test is not here, now, but when he goes back to the States. Will he drink moderately, or completely stop? Will he risk a relapse, and if it occurs to him what will he do? If he stops drinking what alternatives will he find to fill up time, to switch off his mind? Will he make it through the year in that silence, loneliness and snow? Or will he relapse into that night-mare? He must find friends and new things to do. And he must write.

He knows he must be strong, that he has to pull through. He has a wife and three kids and himself to look after. No more taking chances.

Veronica knits him a big woollen sweater. He re-organises the study and clears his drawers and wardrobe of junk and starts pack-ing his bags.

Tindo and Shepherd accompany them to the airport. Veronica slips an envelope into his hand. He hugs them and proceeds to the check-in desk. The plane is waiting, a great white bird ready to chew up distances and transpose him yet again to another culture.

Later on, on the plane, up over the billowing clouds and the shrinking, finicky world, he opens Veronica's card and reads it:

Farai,

You pulled through at the annexe and you'll pull through your life. You're a survivor.

I don't know how to say this, but while you were away in the States and at the annexe, I've grown as a woman, a mother and your friend. I hope you can forgive my shortcomings. I don't know how you'll take this, but I think I can now assume greater charge of my life and I think that's the truest way to start realising oneself and relating to others. I hope you can cope with this and won't be disturbed by it. I sometimes fear you broke down because I developed in your absence. I suspect deep down you are a conservative Shona man, hurting because I grew away from you. The children, Sharai and Ticha especially, are still too young to understand, but one day I'll fully explain to them. I hope you too grew, and grow, out of your experience. We are proud of you. Go well. Work hard and bring us back a book. Who knows, you might live to write about all this one day and educate the world. Find friends and enjoy yourself. Keep yourself busy. Above all learn to love and believe in yourself.

We all love you.

Vee.